LOSING IS NOT AN OPTION

STORIES

LOSING IS NOT AN OPTION

STORIES

RICH WALLACE

ALFRED A. KNOPF NEW YORK

Library of Congress Cataloging-in-Publication Data
Wallace, Rich.
Losing is not an option / by Rich Wallace.
p.   cm.
Summary: Nine episodes in the life of a young man, from sneaking into his tenth football
game in a row with his best friend in sixth grade to running his last high school race,
the Pennsylvania state championships.
ISBN 0-375-81351-9 (trade) — ISBN 0-375-91351-3 (lib. bdg.)
[1. Interpersonal relations—Fiction. 2. Sports—Fiction. 3. Family life—Pennsylvania—Fiction.
4. Pennsylvania—Fiction.] I. Title.

PZ7.W15877 Lo 2003
[Fic]—dc21
2002034036

Printed in the United States of America
August 2003
10 9 8 7 6 5 4 3 2 1
First Edition

FOR PETER JACOBI

Three excellent wishes:

to move the body with grace

to fly without a machine

to outrun time

(FROM "NINE TRIADS" BY LILLIAN MORRISON)

CONTENTS

Night Game

It was the fourth home game of the season, so it'd be ten in a row for us if we could avoid getting nailed going over the fence. We'd gone six for six the year before, in fifth grade, but they'd tightened security that fall.

We dressed dark so we wouldn't be seen, and we knew how to lie in the tall weeds behind the field, timing our move while other kids, less cautious, got caught sneaking in.

We'd never been caught.

I was psyched.

I always walked the four blocks over to Gene's house before the football games, even though my house was closer to the stadium. This was late October, so the sun was down and the sky was barely visible through the maples, broad enough to meet above the street and still holding some red and amber leaves. I needed a sweatshirt under my coat, but no gloves yet. Definitely not a hat.

I walked in the street, right down the middle, rarely having to shift to the sidewalk for a passing car. The traffic to the game was out on Main Street, away from our neighborhood. Most people walked to the games anyway, especially on nights like this.

Gene's house was like ours. I'd walk right in the back door.

His mother would be doing dishes, his father would be reading the paper with a fat cigar in the center of his mouth.

"Ronny's here," Gene's mom would call, and he'd come racing down the stairs.

He'd shoot me a look—No fence can stop us—and go over and kiss his mom.

"Have money?" she asked.

"All I need."

"Pooh-Gene," his dad said, looking up from the paper, "you going to a dance?"

"Huh?"

"Pretty fancy shirt for a football game."

"It'll be under my jacket."

His father just gave him the look—amusement mostly—and nodded as he went back to the paper.

This *was* a little odd, this button-down pinstriped shirt Gene had on. But he grabbed his jacket and kind of pushed his chin toward the door.

"Maybe we'll see you at the game," his mom said. Both sets of our parents would be there (our older brothers sat the bench; they might get in for a few kickoffs in a blowout, but mostly they played on Monday afternoons with the JV squad). If we saw our parents there, we wouldn't let on that we knew them.

Foot traffic was heavy by the time we got to Main Street, and you could feel the banging of the drums six blocks away and the tinny sound of the fight song riding over it.

We turned up Buchanan Street, moving into a darker zone to approach the field from the far corner. "Dickheadsaywhat?" Gene said.

"What?"

He started cracking up.

"You suck," I said, laughing, too. He got me with that a couple of times a week. I smacked him on the arm with my fist.

He stopped walking. "It's a little early yet," he said. "Give it about ten minutes."

We took a seat on the curb. He took a filter-tipped cigar out of his pocket, about the size of a crayon, and stuck it in his mouth.

"Where'd you get that?" I asked.

"Smolinski." His neighbor, a freshman in high school.

He lit the cigar and took a long puff, holding the smoke in his mouth. He handed it to me. The inhalation was surprisingly hot but had a hint of vanilla or something mild.

We both took another puff, then he rubbed it out on the pavement and put it back in his pocket.

"Save that for later," he said.

We'd kicked butt that afternoon, touch football on the street in front of his house. His block had more kids than mine for some reason, and we always managed to get on the same team, whether it was stickball, football, street hockey, or drive-way basketball. There were always other kids around, but we stuck together. We were such close friends with each other that all our other friends seemed peripheral. It was like we shared two homes, two sets of parents, and two older brothers. My parents' photo albums had more pictures of Gene in them than any of my cousins or uncles.

We usually won. He'd hit me with square-outs all the way down the field (telephone poles marking each goal line). We did better than the Giants or the Jets were doing.

Two guys were walking down the hill toward us in a hurry.

Jerry Boyd and Peter Macey. Peter was in the group that had parties and went to the movies with girls. Jerry was his shadow.

"Geno," Peter said as they walked past.

"What's up?" Gene said.

Peter kept walking, turning backward for a few steps. "Going to the game?"

"Eventually."

"See you there."

"Right."

Gene stood up from the curb, wiped off his pants.

"What a jerk," I said, meaning Peter.

"No," Gene said. "He's cool."

"He sure thinks so."

Peter did stupid stuff like writing girls' names on his notebook covers. We didn't want anything to do with that stuff.

"Time to move," Gene said, taking a deep breath. He turned to face me squarely. "Quiet," he said.

"I know." I'd almost screwed it up the week before.

We walked the length of the stadium but a block up the hill from it, then cut through a yard, crossed the gravel parking lot, and made our way down the grassy hill at the corner of the Sturbridge Building Products lot. We edged along through that little patch of woods till we were diagonally across from the refreshment stand, back by that low, shedlike building where they store the pole-vault mats and the lawn tractor.

We knelt there, amid the fallen leaves and stray beer cans, surveying the scene.

Gene nudged my arm. "Falco," he whispered, staring straight ahead.

I looked around. Mr. Falco, a janitor from our school, was

standing inside the fence about fifteen feet from our hopping spot, a place where the barbed wire atop the chain-link fence was cut and hanging and that tractor shed afforded maximum shelter. His back was to us, but it was obvious why he was stationed there. Too many others had been using this spot.

We had alternatives, but we'd need to be quiet. We'd need to risk ripped coats and scratched faces, but we'd get in. We'd save the two bucks' admission.

"Under?" I whispered.

He looked around. "Yeah. Let's go."

I started to get up.

"Wait," he said.

"What?"

"The national anthem's in about five minutes."

"Okay." We slinked back into the shadows.

This was probably the best football team our town had ever had: 6–1 at this point, headed for the play-offs. The quarterback, Mike Esposito, was being recruited by a long list of colleges. He lived five doors up the street from Gene, and you'd see him shooting baskets in his driveway. He'd walk past often, holding hands with his girlfriend, and was always friendly. He claimed he'd received recruiting interest from Notre Dame and Syracuse, but the papers said most of the attention was coming from Division II schools in state, like Kutztown and Bloomsburg. The word in the neighborhood was that he was dumb as a rock.

We could see the band taking formation on the field, light blue uniforms trimmed with darker blue. The overhead lights were brilliant to look at, like staring up at the sun, but all the sound, all the light, was focused on the field. Back where we were was dark, quiet, tense.

The anthem started. We glanced at Mr. Falco, looking out at the field, baseball cap held steadily over his heart. We moved out of the weeds behind the shed, completely shielded from the field. Gene pulled the bottom of the fence toward him. It was loose here; he could lift it ten inches off the ground. I slid under, smelling dirt, and then pushed hard on it, keeping it up so Gene could follow me under. We crouched, waiting for the song to end. We were in.

The trick was to sprint across the fifty yards of practice field between us and the crowd. Then you could blend in over by the bathrooms and the refreshment stand. That was the moment when we could celebrate, slapping hands with each other and laughing.

Gene made a motion with his hand for me to stay low, indicating that we'd try to make our way along the inside of the fence for a ways before darting over. Mr. Falco would never catch us, but there were rent-a-cops on duty and always some teachers milling around eating hot dogs.

The captains were out on the field now for the coin toss, and you could see the cheerleaders with their pom-poms waving and all the players punching shoulder pads and making fists at each other.

The captains jogged off, then the two teams came on for the kickoff. We knew everybody in the stadium was looking at the field.

"Now," he said, and we took off running, pumping our arms and breathing hard. We slowed quickly as we reached the edge of the crowd, separating momentarily as part of the plan and circling around to meet behind the bathrooms.

"Did somebody say ten in a row?" Gene said as I rejoined him. He had a major grin on his face.

"Let's find a seat," I said.

"I gotta hit the bathroom first."

We went in and he started messing with his hair, trying to get it to lay flat. I just gave him a smirk. Who cared what we looked like?

We squeezed in about six rows up, down by the twenty-yard line. My heart was still pumping.

We scored on our first possession, Esposito rolling out, looking toward the end zone. Lenny Hill had a step on his defender, thirty yards up the field, but Esposito tucked the ball in, cut toward the sideline, and simply outran everybody for the touchdown.

We jumped to our feet and yelled. The band started up. Esposito ran off the field, took off his helmet, and walked to the bench for some water. He stood there, acting like he was oblivious to the crowd, but he was soaking it all in.

A pack of guys our age and a little older walked by at the bottom of the bleachers, wearing their junior football team jerseys. Tracy Jackson and Gwen Monahan were trailing behind them, scanning the bleachers as they walked.

Tracy waved when she saw Gene. I glanced over at him; he gave Tracy a barely noticeable nod.

She put up two fingers and kind of beckoned him, but he didn't go. She pointed toward the upper row of bleachers, ahead toward the fifty-yard line or so, then smiled and they kept on walking.

We were two touchdowns ahead by halftime. Gene and I took great pride in never watching the band perform at the half, so we made our way over to buy candy and flat Coke.

I got a Mounds bar and looked around. Tracy and Gwen and

some others were over by the fence, looking at us. At Gene, anyway. He looked at them, then back at me. "Come on," he said, turning to walk toward the bathrooms again.

The men's room was crowded, guys lined up four deep at the urinals. Gene went over to the sink, messed with his hair again. I got on one of the lines.

He exhaled kind of heavily, then blinked a couple of times. "I'll meet you out there," he said.

I took my time. Even washed my hands. When I came out Gene was over by those girls. He and Tracy were standing a little apart from the group, maybe thirty feet from where I was standing. Then Tracy was walking toward me.

"Hi, Ronny," she said.

"Hi."

"Good game, huh?" She and I'd been friendly back in second grade, but she'd veered off into popularity long ago. I didn't know what to make of this sudden friendliness. I could see Gene with his back to me, talking to Franny Haines, who was a couple of inches taller than he was and had breasts already. I guess Tracy had some, too.

She said something else, but I wasn't listening.

"Ronny?" she said.

"Yeah."

"Give Gene a few minutes, okay?"

I could have told her that Gene didn't have any interest in what Franny had to offer and that he didn't want to hang out with anybody but me. But I figured I'd let her find that out for herself.

I watched Tracy walk away, looked back at Gene and Franny, and walked slowly toward the end-zone fence. From there I could watch the marching band. I tried to ignore Gene and Franny, but I couldn't help looking over a few times.

Gene came over just before halftime ended, as the teams made their way out of the locker rooms.

"Let's go," he said, and we walked back to our spot in the bleachers.

I wanted to ask what that was all about, but I didn't. We did the usual second-half routine, yelling every time we scored or made a big gain, but Gene seemed distracted. I felt little and young. Like a sixth grader.

"I told her I'd walk her home," he said when the game ended. "You wanna meet me over by Turkey Hill?"

"I guess so. When?"

"Give me twenty minutes," he said. "Maybe a half hour."

"Okay." I stayed in the bleachers while everybody filed out, watching Gene push his way through the crowd. I caught sight of him and Franny leaving through the gate, with Tracy and Gwen and some others following about twenty feet behind.

I made my way up to street level. I could see Mike Esposito and the head coach out in front of the locker room, talking to a couple of men in ties who were writing in notebooks. Esposito had his jersey and shoulder pads off, and the dark T-shirt he was wearing was soaked and sticking to his skin.

I moved away from the crowd, heading back to my neighborhood, reversing the way we'd come earlier.

Franny lived somewhere uphill and to the left, so I made my way down to Main Street in a hurry. Horns were beeping, celebrating the win, and crowds were gathering at the two pizza places in town. Usually we'd be making noise, too, like we were a big part of that win even though all we did was yell from the bleachers. That night I felt kind of hollow and alone.

I walked over to Church Street, out of my way, and took my

time heading up toward the Turkey Hill store. I'd get another candy bar. I'd wait.

Church Street is just a block in from Main, running parallel. It was empty and dark. I could hear the river, one block to my right, and had a better look at the sky.

The fence-hopping streak had reached double figures that night. Ten in a row. This had been the toughest one yet. Or at least it had looked like it would be. It had actually been pretty easy. No less of a rush, though. Next time we'd probably pay the two dollars.

We were scheduled to meet at nine the next morning for football—Gene, Louie, the Hernandez brothers. In a couple of weeks we'd switch to basketball, then street hockey when the snow came. Stickball as soon as it thawed.

Ten in a row was a nice solid number. Like a photograph to keep in an album, or like something slippery that I'd try my best to hold on to.

Nailed

I've never liked this guy Gary. I barely knew him before this year because he went to the Catholic school through sixth grade and lives on the other side of town. But we're rivals anyway. Both of us small, both into sports, both of us the fastest one in our schools.

I'd see him at the swimming pool and played against him in Little League and YMCA sports, and he told me to eat shit a couple of times and I told him where to shove it. So we knew each other's reputations when we got to the middle school. His team beat ours in the Y soccer championships last year, and he made me look bad all game.

It pissed me off when he made the basketball team and I didn't. I outplayed him in the tryouts, but the coach—our gym teacher—thinks Gary is hot shit. There's no way he deserved to make the team over me.

I don't mind getting cut. It happens. But to keep a slimy little guy like that over me totally sucks.

So I plan to kick his ass up and down the court today, my first chance to show him up in a real basketball game. This is the Jaycees league at the Y—Saturday afternoons, seventh and eighth graders. We're 3–2 and they're undefeated, but as far as I'm concerned, it's just me versus Gary.

"Gonna nail you, Ron," he says as he walks past me during warm-ups.

"We'll see," I tell him, meaning *You'll* see, jerk.

"We'll see, all right," he says. He sneers at me, turns to one of his buddies, and says, "He actually thinks they can beat us."

Somehow four of the kids from the middle school basketball team wound up on Gary's team in this league, so they've dominated all their games. Our team is mostly small, quiet guys, but we play together pretty well. I play point guard and I take that seriously, so I don't do a lot of scoring. Our inside guys can put it in the hoop if I get it to them.

The game starts and Gary is showing off on the first possession, dribbling the ball between his legs and talking a lot. Girls he hangs around with and some of his other friends are watching from the bleachers, egging him on. I hate guys like Gary who need a posse around them.

I cover him tight, hands up. He tries to drive past me, but I keep between him and the basket. Finally he picks up his dribble and I really hound him, and he throws the ball to one of our guys.

I get the ball and dribble up fast, with Gary right on me. I hit Eddie in the corner and he fakes a shot, ducks under his man, and gives me a perfect bounce pass as I drive to the basket. I'm a step up on Gary and I lay the ball off the backboard into the hoop.

I don't think my teammates were intimidated by these guys, but this basket seems to give them some extra confidence. Our defense is great through the quarter, and we build a six-point lead with patient play. I get a steal from Gary and go the length of the court for another layup just before the buzzer, and we're up 12–4 after one.

"You're dead meat, Ron," he says as we walk off the court.

I just point at the scoreboard.

He comes out seething and makes a terrible pass to start the quarter. Eddie smothers the pass and elbows big Jimmy, their center, and I race over to get the ball. "Stay smart," I say as I dribble upcourt.

We do that through the second quarter. Gary is not a great dribbler; I can tie him up way outside and make him give up the ball. He does some grabbing and shoving, just enough not to get called, and keeps up a steady stream of insults under his breath. I hold him scoreless and he throws a couple more away. By half-time we're up 25–13, and Jimmy and their other frontcourt guys are getting on Gary for screwing up.

In this league everybody has to sit at least one full quarter, so I watch the third from the bench. So does Gary. We glare over at each other. His cool friends and the girls don't mean anything on the basketball court.

They manage to cut the lead to seven, but that's good enough for me.

"Prime time," Gary says as he dribbles in place above the key. "Now you get nailed," he says.

I nod, give him a beckoning motion with my fingers. He jumps and shoots, missing badly, and my teammate Louie comes down with the rebound and races up the court. He passes to Eddie, who crosses midcourt and finds me again. I don't need to break stride, taking the ball into the lane, stepping left, and pivoting. Gary fouls me badly, but he argues the call.

I make both free throws.

"Let's press," I say, and Louie covers the guy making the in-bounds pass. I stick tight to Gary, who takes the pass and lets his elbow fly. It grazes my arm. Nothing. He dribbles up fast, doesn't even look to pass. Just sets up for a three-pointer and shoots it. Not close.

Our coach yells, "Take your time" to me as I bring up the ball. (The coaches in this league are mostly high school and college kids; ours is a freshman at King's.) He's right. We're up nine with seven minutes left, and Gary is obviously panicking.

Their whole team seems tight, confused. We move the ball around. They're going for steals, overplaying on defense, and eventually I find Eddie wide open underneath for a layup.

The lead grows to fifteen while Gary's team takes hurried shots and hardly bothers passing. Gary is 0 for 11 by my count when he finally hits a wild three with two minutes left in the game.

"In your face!" he says, and I just laugh. We're still ahead by a dozen.

Coach pulls our starters with about a minute left, and we walk off beaming, slapping hands and shouting. When it ends we shake hands with the other team, but Gary isn't in line.

I head down to the locker room, and he's in there with two of his friends. I've got Louie with me, which is better than nobody.

"Way to nail me, Gary," I say. This is beautiful.

"Yeah?" he says, making a fist. "Want me to nail you right now?"

"Sure."

"I'll trash you, Ron."

"I'm waiting."

"Any time, pal."

I just stand there, waiting for him to move. He glares at me. Calls me an asshole.

"What are you waiting for?" I ask.

He turns toward the outside door. "We'll play you again," he says.

"Three weeks," I say. "I've got it circled on my calendar."

"I'll kick your ass," he says as he steps outside into the parking lot.

I follow him out. When he's twenty feet away, he turns and gives me the finger. "You're dead," he says.

"I'm waiting."

I lean against the building and watch him walk away.

Think you're tougher than I am?

Prove it.

The Amazing Two-Headed Boy

My father won a third-place ribbon at the county fair thirty years ago for his 4-H goat, back when that meant something. Third out of hundreds. Last year we sat in the empty grandstand one Thursday afternoon and watched nine goats get judged. The only entries. My father didn't have much to say.

We live in town. Dad left the farm years ago and never looked back. There are fewer farms around now. More people.

Later in the week I'll spend an evening here with my mom and dad, maybe go to the demolition derby, but on opening night I need to roam. So me and Louie walked along Route 191 the mile or so to the fairgrounds, paid the six dollars to get in, and got our hands stamped in case we decide to leave and come back. In case we meet somebody, for example.

We start looking.

In particular I am looking for girls. Having Louie along will probably not help in the search—he's tall and skinny and awkward and talks with a lisp—but it's better than doing it alone.

I am, at best, in the second tier among my classmates, nowhere near the elite level, where guys and girls have been pairing up since fifth grade, talking on the phone, instant-messaging each other, and having parties where they make out and smoke. Those are not the people I am looking for.

Just inside the entrance to the fairgrounds are rows and rows of vendors selling T-shirts and jewelry and leather stuff and rubbery necklaces that glow in the dark in red and green and orange. And you're hit right away with the smells of pizza and french fries and London-broil sandwiches. There's country line dancing going on at the small stage outside the farm museum, watched by a cluster of old people and tiny little kids.

Louie is a year and a half older than I am, but we'll both be eighth graders this fall. Tonight he's got several welts on his arm and another on his neck.

"Got stung," he says. "Catching hornets . . . in the dumpster behind the diner."

"Oh," I say.

"Caught a really big one."

We go into the pavilion where they have the vegetable and pie exhibits. We look at the cucumbers first. They all look pretty much the same.

There are piles of small green apples. Most apples don't ripen until fall—I know that much—but these have already been judged, so there are ribbons by some of the piles. They've judged the string beans and tomatoes, too. Louie picks up a zucchini, looks around, and says, "Ron" to draw my attention. He holds the squash down by his crotch and smirks at me.

"Right," I say. "Try a string bean."

The other side of the pavilion has paintings and photographs and other artwork. Most of it's by younger kids, but I see that a girl I sat next to in English last year won second prize for a photo of a deer with two spotted fawns. Angie Callahan. I talked to her once. She dropped a pen. I picked it up and said, "Here." She said, "Thanks." That was back in February. Maybe I'll run into her tonight.

We get Cokes at a fish-and-chips stand. Way too much ice, but it's a big cup. We reach the carnival midway, with the rides and games. The crowd is so thick you get jostled every step. They've got all the kiddie rides like flying Dumbos and a miniature train right here by the grandstand. The Big-Rig Truck Pull is going on in the arena.

I stop and look at the little kids bouncing in one of those big caged-in air-mattress things. When I turn back, Louie is talking to two couples our age, the girls both wearing little halter things and the guys with choker beads and cool haircuts. Ricky Butler acknowledges me, but the girls look kind of bored and don't make eye contact. Louie can talk to anybody, but I know what they say behind his back.

Ricky and the others go into the truck pull. We keep going toward the better rides.

I've got a Knicks shirt on, so naturally the guy at the basketball shoot calls me over and starts busting my chops. "Two balls for a dollar. You got a dollar?"

"Maybe. You got two balls?"

"Wiseass."

He's a college guy, or at least the age of one. I know they've got the rims bent so you have to make a perfect shot, but I'm up for it. If I make them both I win a basketball.

My first shot hits hard against the back of the rim and drops off, but the second one swishes. The guy hands me a plastic whistle and says I should try again. Maybe later.

"Candy!" Louie says, and we step over to the booth where

you can win fifty bars at a time. Of course they paint the 50 BARS thing in huge letters on the wheel, but they angle it so there's only a tiny fraction of the wheel that would actually give you that prize.

I put a quarter on the seven and Louie plays five. We lose twice each before five comes up, and the guy tosses a little ticket thing toward Louie as he sweeps up the quarters.

"It says four bars," Louie says.

"That's decent," I say.

"Maybe we can sell 'em and make some of my money back."

He gets four Hershey bars, smaller than the ones you buy at the store. He shoves them into his back pocket with his wallet.

We head toward the animal sheds, which are over in the far corner of the grounds. We pass crowds of kids our age and younger, and some older. Kids come from over by Wallenpaupack or even Scranton for this, and of course there are lots of out-of-towners in the area in the summer. New Yorkers and people from Jersey. They have summer homes.

My father says the fair gets worse every year. More New Jersey sleazebags, more gold jewelry, more loudmouths. Fewer sheep and cattle.

Jared Osborne walks up to us eating a sausage sandwich. We're friends. I used to kick his butt at everything sportswise, but last winter he grew about six inches and sprouted muscles and facial hair, and this spring he was the best sprinter on our track team, including the eighth graders. I was about third. Maybe fourth.

"What are you guys doing?" Jared asks.

"Hanging around," Louie says. "Maybe get in a fight later."

"For what?"

"No reason. Just if somebody says something I don't like."

"Oh."

I look at Louie, then at Jared. "What are you doing?" I ask.

"Looking for Nick."

Nick is at the top of the elite group. He mostly hangs with high school kids and has a new girlfriend every week. Jared's gone from below us to way ahead in a matter of months. That happens.

Jared walks away. We're by the freak show, and the signs say TWO-HEADED COW, WORLD'S FATTEST MAN, BEARDED LADY, MONKEY BOY. It's the same show they have every year. You go inside the tent (for three dollars) and they have *pictures* of a bearded lady and a two-headed cow and other things. They have a real dead python with two heads, but it's pretty obvious the second head was sewn on.

There *is* a very huge man in there who needs a cart to get around, but it's hard to imagine that he's the world's fattest. I get the idea that the pictures and the snake and stuff belong to him. Anyway, we reach the stables where the 4-H animals are kept. Kids camp out here to be by their animals in the days before the judging, grooming them and feeding them and cleaning the stalls. Most of the animals aren't here yet; mainly it's just some cows, but the barn smells good, like hay and cow manure.

There are about six horses that live here year-round. They're in their stalls. I go up to one and pat its nose, a dark brown guy with a white spot on his forehead.

This end of the fairgrounds is still quiet, since most of the livestock stuff doesn't begin for a few days. So when we turn toward another stall we're surprised to see two girls sitting on the ground smoking cigarettes. They're about, what—maybe eighteen? They both have blue T-shirts that say GRANDSTAND AMUSEMENTS, so they must be with the carnival.

"Taking a break?" Louie says.

"Been working hard," says the one with red hair. She's got the bottom of her shirt rolled up and tied above her navel. The other one has shortish dark hair with maroon tips, and one of those fluorescent orange necklaces wrapped a couple of times around her wrist. "Came to see the horses," she says.

I look at the horse in the stall she's sitting by, a lighter-colored one with a blondish mane.

"So what are you boys up to?" the red-haired one asks. "Looking for trouble?"

"We make trouble," Louie says. "We don't need to look for it."

Good one, Louie. I'm sure they're impressed.

The red-haired one uncrosses her legs. "Wow," she says. "We better look out, Deb."

Deb laughs. She gets up and leans against the wall, taking a deep drag on her cigarette. "So. You guys local?" she says.

"Not really," Louie says. "We've lived all over. My dad travels a lot. Racing cars. So we move around. We just live here for now."

Louie is full of shit. His dad works at Sturbridge Building Products and they've lived here a hundred years.

Deb looks right past him at me and licks her lips. She stares at me for a few seconds. I feel like I'm going to melt.

"Racing cars," she says. "Wow. What about you?" she asks me. "You play for the Knicks?"

I laugh. "Sure."

"Show her the whistle," Louie says. "He won it shooting baskets."

"You must be quite a shooter," Deb says. She's no taller than I am. Looks like she's got strong arms and could kick my butt. She's kind of staring me down now. "See that trailer?" she finally says, motioning with her head toward a blue-and-white trailer behind the Tilt-A-Whirl.

"Yeah?" My voice sounds kind of squeaky.

"Got twenty bucks?" she asks. She runs her tongue back and forth across her teeth.

Louie giggles. "Holy shit," he says.

The red-haired one is standing now, too. "Same deal for you," she tells Louie. "Or would that be *too much* trouble?"

"Shit," he says again, drawing out the word. He looks at me with a grin and very wide eyes. He's blushing. My mouth feels dry.

"Geez," I say under my breath. I should laugh, too, but all I can manage is a weak, wimpy "Heh." I have at least that much in my wallet.

Louie swallows hard. "I've got two dollars and four Hershey bars," he says.

The red-haired one snorts. "Take a hike," she says. She gives him a good hard stare. "Get lost. Send your race-car father instead."

Louie backs away, looking at me, looking like a scared little kid. I take a step back, too. Deb tilts her head to the side, then back, studying me. I can't move. "Go take a Dumbo ride, fellas." They both crack up. I feel smaller than a string bean.

We don't say a word as we hurry out of the barn and make our way through the crowd again, past the bumper cars and the merry-go-round and the Italian-ice stand and bingo. The truck pull is still going on, and there's a rock band playing near the entrance.

Jared goes by with two girls I don't recognize, both of them showing lots of suntanned skin and smelling overly sweet. They look five years older than us but probably aren't at all.

Louie stares after them with his mouth open, then bites down on his lip. "How much money you have?" he finally says.

"A few bucks," I say. "Maybe forty," though I don't think I have quite that much left.

"Can you loan me some?" he asks. "Just a dollar so I can get in the freak show. I'll pay you back next week."

"Sure," I say. "No problem."

"You want a candy bar?" he asks.

"Yeah," I say as we walk past the basketball shoot. "Later we'll win fifty more."

I Voted
for Mary Ann

Last night my dad hassled me about staying out late every night
this week and only working part-time. I said it's August, I'm in
training. I run every evening and I hang out to unwind. I get up
early to run again, and I can only handle so much. So twenty-
five hours a week washing dishes is all I can stand right now. He
said I was a pussy.

So I was lying in bed thinking of how all we do is disagree
anymore. And I thought about Grandpa, and how he used to
show up every Sunday when we were little, laughing and joking and carrying pies and rolls from the bakery, and he'd give
me and Devin money and take us bowling and out to Pizza
Hut. And when I was eleven and I did a crappy job painting
his porch and I knew it and I cried about it, he called me the
next morning and told me to come back and see how great it
looked now that the paint had dried and smoothed itself out.
And we both knew he'd touched it up himself, but we never
said so. He just made me feel good about it.

My grandfather died four years ago. One afternoon soon
after Grandma had sold his building, we were in there putting
things in boxes and sending his desk and other office furniture

to an auction house and cleaning up for the new owner when I came across a key in one of the filing cabinets with a piece of brown cord tied through the hole.

I was twelve, so I went around fitting the key into keyholes to try to find a match for it. Turned out it was for the back door. I slipped it into my pocket and took it home.

In my grandfather's time he sold insurance on the main floor, just him and a secretary and a phone and a typewriter—no computer or fax machine or anything like that.

Upstairs was a one-bedroom apartment he'd left vacant for a year or so since the ninety-seven-year-old previous tenant had moved to her daughter's. Grandpa said she'd been costing him more in heat than he made in rent, which he hadn't had the heart to raise in twenty-six years. Old ladies never seem to be warm enough.

Above the apartment is a little slope-ceilinged attic area where Grandpa stored paperwork and broken lamps, and a tinier bathroom with a medicine cabinet above the sink where he kept a toothbrush and mouthwash and a razor and a photo of his only child, my mom. There was a bigger bathroom on the main floor, of course, but he left that for his secretary to use.

Grandpa'd been doing business more or less the same way for over forty years. The end came suddenly—shoveling snow in his driveway at home.

The building, on Ninth Street just down from Main, is brick and small and shares its walls with a dentist's office and a barber. It has a tiny backyard—mostly cement, but with just enough dirt for a decrepit old apple tree and a decorative metal pedestal that might have served as a table some generations ago. You can only get to the yard by going out the back door or by cutting through the bank's parking lot and climbing over a green picket fence.

They've got a 1907 photo of the building over at the Sturbridge Historical Society and it doesn't look much different.

These days a mortgage broker operates out of the main floor, and the apartment upstairs has been converted into an accountant's office. Entering the back door after midnight does not yield access to either office, but it does permit you to take the narrow staircase to the attic. From all appearances, I am the only one who ever goes up there.

Last night I couldn't sleep after the argument with my father, so I got up and sneaked outside and walked along Church Street to the bank's parking lot and looked around. It was one-thirty; no one was out. Grandpa's building was dark, as usual. So I hopped the fence and looked around again. And then I unlocked the door and walked upstairs.

There's always a chill in the attic and spiderwebs in the corners. The ceiling is thick wooden beams and planks; fat nails hammered partway in here and there. There's one bare sixty-watt bulb with a pull cord in the center of the space, but I've never dared to see if it works. I always carry a flashlight and mute it with my hand.

I've tried the bathroom water and it still comes on, coughing and sputtering at first and running a rusty brown for a minute. I don't touch the toothbrush or the razor, just look at them and at the photo of my mom at about thirteen taped to the inside of the cabinet. There's a radiator my grandfather painted silver the summer before he died, but the rust is showing through.

The attic and bathroom have been undisturbed in the years since he left, unused by the new owner. Fat guy; can't see him climbing all those stairs. This was Grandpa's domain for almost half a century, and I think it still is. But how long can that last? When I miss him the most I come here.

I taped a poem for my grandfather next to that picture of my mom, just eight short lines about him being the nicest person I'll ever know.

I stepped out of the bathroom and flashed the light around the attic, hitting the shutters leaning against the bricks, a couple of ancient screens for the downstairs windows, and a heavy white door lying on its side, coated in dust, FOR BETW. UPSTAIR BEDRM AND BATH penciled on it in Grandpa's block printing.

And then the light caught something I'd never noticed before, sticking out just slightly from the eaves. I reached up and pulled down a fat old magazine and immediately saw it was a *Playboy*. Old. December 1965. It was in pretty good shape. I wiped the dust from the cover with my sleeve and rested the magazine on the floor, kneeling with the light in my left hand while I turned the pages with my right.

I wondered, When was the last time Grandpa looked at this? Back in '65? Or did he make regular visits? Maybe there were some others stashed around up there.

I kept turning pages, and soon I came across an unmistakable face. No question about it. Ginger. From *Gilligan's Island*. Good and naked.

I laughed a little and stared. Kept staring. There were other photo spreads, but I kept going back to that one.

I had to share it with the boys.

I've seen every episode at least six times; the reruns are on continuously.

So I took it with me; it was the first time I've removed anything on any of my late-night visits. And I had it with me when I went over to Kevin's house the next night, and I had it with me when we went down to Turkey Hill.

Tony always said he'd take Mary Ann over Ginger any day if he'd been cast away on that island. I tended to agree with him, but Kevin was a hard-core Ginger fan. He went nuts when I showed him the photo spread, and I had to push him away to keep him from slobbering on the pages.

"Not bad," Tony said when confronted with the evidence.

"Right," said Kevin. "You'd rather sleep with the Skipper."

"Don't think so."

"Or Mrs. Howell."

Other guys came over and we eventually voted 6–3 in favor of Ginger, based primarily on those photos. I got pissed when the cover ripped as this jerk Alex grabbed for it and Kevin wouldn't let go. I said, "Enough already. This is valuable."

"The women in that magazine are like a hundred years old now," Tony said. "Remember that when you're under the sheets tonight, Ron."

"Nice math," I said. "They aren't even retired yet."

"Where'd you get that, anyway?" Kevin asked.

"Used-book store over in Hawley," I lied. "They got lots of 'em. Now give me that," I said, taking a firm hold on it and bonking him with my free hand. "Assholes. Leave it alone."

I left the bench soon after that and walked along Church Street by myself. It was only quarter after ten, too early to sneak into the attic. But I was going to put it back there that night. None of those jerks would ever get their grimy hands on my grandfather's stuff again. I shouldn't have messed with it, either.

So I went home and went up to my room and lay on the

bed with the radio on softly and stared at the ceiling in the dark.

I dozed off, but I'd set my watch to beep at one A.M. When it woke me I put on my running shoes and a dark sweatshirt and quietly left the house with the magazine held against my skin.

And as I took those stairs I felt scared for the first time; scared that I'd get caught maybe, that I'd spoil this scene forever and they'd clean up Grandpa's domain. So I climbed the stairs even more slowly than usual, careful not to let them creak, and cupped my hand more tightly over the flashlight's beam.

I put the magazine back where I'd found it, but I hid it better than he had. And I looked around the attic for a good long time, seeing it as I always did, but more clearly maybe, more aware.

And I went in the bathroom and picked up the toothbrush and turned it over in my hand and touched my mother's photo, smelled the razor, touched the faucets.

I took a couple of deep breaths and whispered, "Sorry I disturbed things, Grandpa. I love you." I turned and made my way down the stairs.

And I feel kind of empty now as I walk toward home, the river gurgling a block away, the lights of Main Street the same distance away on my other side. I've got a crystal-clear picture of the attic in my head, and the smell of the place to go with it. The pattern of rust in the sink and the white linoleum peeling up around the toilet, the old knob-and-tube wiring stapled to the beams, the single hook inside the bathroom door where he used to hang his shirt while he shaved, the yellowed bristles of

his toothbrush, the crud on his razor, the dead flies in the corner, the silence.

How long can a place remain the same? Maybe forever, if
you leave it alone. I'll keep the key, but I know I can't go back.

I know I can't risk it again.

In Letters That Would Soar a Thousand Feet High

We were charging up that last hill coming out of the woods and this is where he always seemed to finish me off, the final three hundred yards or so. But today I found an extra lift and I could feel him straining. Perfect October day—bright sunshine, crisp air, and the smell of wet leaves on the ground. We'd dropped everybody else by the midway point and it was just Smith and me pushing it, and it was one of those races with no gaps of effort, no easing up on the downhills or saving anything for a kick. That last climb up the narrow winding path before you burst out of the maples and onto the grass and into the open toward the finish line, that's when I finally broke him, when I couldn't help turning it into an early sprint and building a gap of a couple of yards that kept growing.

I could still hear him breathing, hear his feet hitting the ground and the squall of the spectators, knowing they'd be surprised to see me first out of the woods. Then the all-out sprint across the field, brushing the grass, no pain at all this time, just a rush and a charge and a league championship and a win over this guy I'd been chasing since middle school.

He grabbed my arm in the chute and said, "Nice race" and I turned and nodded and said, "About time I got you." He squeezed his thumb a little harder into my bicep and said he'd figured I'd get him sometime.

Coach came over and gave me a bear hug and said I finally put it all together. I watched my teammates finish and yelled for the ones who were close to other runners. Then I walked back toward the woods and when I got there I pumped my fist and shouted, "Yes!" although I barely let it come out above a whisper.

I gave myself a minute alone to let it sink in, then jogged back across the field toward our pile of sweats and stuff.

Denny Smith goes to Weston North. He's the defending district cross-country champion and placed fourth in the 3,200 at the state track meet last spring. A month before at the Scranton Invitational I'd given him a race to the finish, and then in the dual meet a week later the same thing happened; he just sat on my butt and outkicked me down the stretch.

People from our girls' team were telling me Nice-race Nice-race Way-to-go-Ron when Smith jogged up to me and asked if I wanted to cool down. I said yeah and took off my jersey and put on a long-sleeved T-shirt I'd ordered from L. L. Bean. It was a warm day, but I like sweating; he was just in his shorts and had a thin chain around his neck and I could tell the girls were checking him out, the ripped abs and the tan and the lean wiriness and the smile, but they're mostly shy like I am.

So we jogged around the perimeter of the field and talked about training and I said I'd been doing a bit of track work in the evenings, just eight 200s a couple of times a week, and that seemed to be paying off. He said he'd be doing a lot of speed work over the next two weeks to get ready for the states and wouldn't be doing any more weight work until winter.

He came up to me again after the medal ceremony.

"Listen," he said. "There's a great party over near your way tonight. You want to go?"

"Sure," I said. I didn't know of any parties this weekend except a rumor of a closed one at a cheerleader's house. Didn't know how he'd know about that.

"It's in a barn off Owego Road. Friend of my cousin. I'll be going through Sturbridge. Pick you up?"

"Yeah. Should I tell these other guys?" My teammates.

He tightened up his mouth, moved his head from side to side. "Might be better not to. It's kind of a small space and I don't think I should bring a crowd."

"Got ya," I said. "Tell you what. I'll be out on Main Street by eight o'clock. We hang down by the Turkey Hill store."

"I know the place. I'll pick you up like eight-thirty, quarter to nine."

"Great."

I see him pull up in a blue pickup truck and turn the corner, easing to a stop on the side street. I'm standing with Kevin and Tony in back of the bench finishing a pack of Twinkies, scraping the excess off the cardboard with my teeth.

"I'm taking off," I say. "I'll see you guys tomorrow."

"Don't be a faggot," Kevin says. "It's only like eight-thirty."

"I'm not going home, slime," I say. "I gotta go somewhere. I might be back."

"You suck."

Smith's standing outside his truck with the door open and the motor running. He's got his hair gelled and he's dressed better than any of us ever are—gray sweater, a belt, leather shoes.

"Hey," he says.

"Hey."

I get in the truck and he says, "Great race today, Ron."

"Thanks. You, too."

I've never hung out with anybody from another town before, so this feels kind of life-expanding. I've gotten to know Smith somewhat over the years. Cross-country and track are like that—you almost can't help getting to know your opponents because you aren't hidden behind a helmet and you have time after the races to talk. But my social life has never crossed the Sturbridge border before.

We drive past Turkey Hill and I give Tony and Kevin and the others a nod and they look at me like Where the hell are *you* going?

"So where's this party?" I ask.

"A few miles out of town," he says. "It's mostly college people. Should be fun. Last time I went out there they had a karaoke machine. I mean, the barn is all fixed up—it's not like there's cows living in it. It's like an underage club. Some guys from the U of Scranton run it. Like I said, a friend of my cousin is behind it."

"Sounds cool."

"I think you'll like it."

We turn off 191 onto Owego Road and head toward Waymart. After a few miles he turns onto a narrow dirt road and slows down a lot to avoid bottoming out in the ruts. He's been playing a Garth Brooks tape and I haven't said anything about it, but my friends would not ever let me hear the end of it if I played anything like that around them. Not that I would anyway. But I bear it and figure maybe this is some kind of country-western place we're headed to and he's getting into the spirit.

I can see a barn up ahead with some light coming from it, and we pull onto a grassy field near a couple of dozen other vehicles. "You don't need to lock it," he says.

Sounds like old disco music playing; the Bee Gees, I think. It's a clear night, a lot cooler than at race time, with lots of stars.

There's a guy at the barn door in a baseball cap, with a scruffy goatee. "Hey, love," he says to Smith.

"Jerry," Smith says.

"Five tonight."

"Okay. I'll pay for my buddy. This is Ron," he says, motioning to me with his hand.

"Hi," the guy says to me. "Thanks, sweetie," he says to Smith, who's handing him a ten-dollar bill.

Sweetie? Give me a break.

"Thanks," I say to Smith. "I didn't know there was a cover."

"For the DJ and the kegs," he says.

The barn is lit by several bare lightbulbs hanging from wires, so it's kind of dim. And it does have the lingering aroma of cows. There are hay bales stacked against the walls, but mostly it's a big empty space with a dirt floor. I'd say there are forty-five people here, most of them guys between eighteen and twenty-two or so.

"Beer?" Smith says.

"Sure."

I scan the room for girls and see a handful, but this looks mostly like a drinking and laughing situation. I'd been hoping I might meet somebody. You never know. It's early; more women may show up later.

The DJ is about twenty and he's got his cap on backward and he's dancing in place to the Supremes with his fists up about chest level, rotating his body back and forth, and a cigarette hanging from his lips. The kegs are set up to his right and are labeled COORS LIGHT and YUENGLING. We get big plastic cups of Yuengling. Smith introduces me to a couple of people.

"Wendy, Steve, this is Ron."

Wendy is kind of overweight and Steve looks sort of girlish; no shoulders, perfect hair, a red ribbed turtleneck sweater.

"These guys graduated from North last spring," Smith says. "We worked on the school paper."

"Nice to meet you," Wendy says. Steve doesn't say anything. "Where you from?"

"Sturbridge," I say. We have to shout a bit because the music is loud in here. "I know Denny from cross-country."

"Oh, you're the one," she says. She gives Smith a little smile and flicks up her eyebrows. She must have heard that I beat him today.

"Twist and Shout" comes on and Wendy says to Steve, "We gotta dance to this."

He agrees, sort of reluctantly, and they move toward the center of the barn.

"Steve was so afraid to come here," Smith says.

"How come?"

"He's just petrified. Wendy finally got him to come, but only if she promised to come with him."

"She's his girlfriend?"

"No. No, they've been friends since like kindergarten. But no . . . she's, she kind of gives him confidence or something."

About fifteen more people have arrived, so the place is filling up fast. A big guy in an LJC Wrestling T-shirt comes up and grabs Smith's shoulders from behind and shakes him. Smith turns with a grin and says, "You butthead. What's up? How's school?"

"Great. Parties every night. You'll see, next year." He looks around.

Smith motions with his chin toward Wendy and Steve. The wrestling guy nods.

"This is Ron," Smith says.

The guy shakes my hand hard. "What's going on, Ron?"

"Nothing much. Just hanging out."

"Any karaoke yet?" he asks Smith.

"Nah. The place is just filling up now. You performing?"

"Absolutely," he says. "As soon as I get a few beers in me."

"What are you doing?"

"Hell, I don't know. Something funny. I was working on a few things all week. You'll see." He sticks his arm straight out and points at the kegs and starts walking that way with his arm still sticking out.

Smith turns to me. "Marv's a riot. Last time he did 'Paradise by the Dashboard Light' with some girl he knows from school. You know, that old Meat Loaf song."

"Must have been funny."

"The karaoke is a blast. You'll see."

An hour later the place is packed and there's been a steady stream of guys doing songs by macho country people like George Strait, Alan Jackson, and Travis Tritt, plus insipid versions of "After the Loving" and "To Sir, With Love," but the crowd is rowdy and everybody's laughing. I've just been hanging back, leaning against the wall and drinking beer. Wendy and Steve and Marv the wrestling guy are with us, but we can't talk much because they've upped the volume a lot. Wendy has been talking to me between songs and keeps running her thumb down my sleeve. She's got curly brown hair and bright red lipstick. Smith seems to be fostering communication between Marv and Steve. I don't know why those two would have any interest in each other; Marv is a loud party animal and Steve looks like he could gently flap his wings and float toward the ceiling. So Steve and Marv are talking to Smith and looking across at each other. I'm guessing that Steve likes Marv. I'm also guessing that Marv would beat the shit out of him if he tried anything.

"All right, I'm ready," Marv says after a while, and starts working his way through the crowd toward the DJ.

Apparently he has a reputation, because he gets applause even before he starts singing. He gives a big embarrassed grin and shakes his head. Then he raises his hand for quiet and the song begins.

"You don't bring me flowers," he sings in a high girly voice that doesn't sound a lot like Barbra Streisand, "you don't sing me love songs. . . ."

But then he changes his voice, and he really does sound like Neil Diamond: "You hardly talk to me anymore, when I come through the door at the end . . . of . . . the . . . day."

The crowd goes nuts. He does the whole song like that, doing both voices of the duet, and people are yelling for more.

"Later, boys," he says, and hands the microphone back to the DJ.

Wendy pokes my arm. "You gonna sing?"

"No. I suck. Are you?"

"Sure. It's easy. You just have to pick something upbeat or funny. It's a rush, believe me."

"She's good." The first words Steve has said to me. Marv has made his way back and Steve smiles over at him. "Nice," he says. Marv smiles back, blushing a bit. I wince a little and look around.

Another guy is up there doing "This Magic Moment," standing kind of sideways with his eyes closed and his elbow up at a right angle, holding the mike steady. Steve kind of rotates his shoulders in a little dance, squinting at Marv, who's got a sweaty forehead from singing.

"I'm going up," Wendy says.

"You go, girl," says Smith.

She has to wait while two guys do the "Summer Nights" duet from *Grease*. Wendy does "Passionate Kisses" and she can go pretty good. Quite a few people are dancing now.

I turn and see Steve smoking a cigarette, holding it awkwardly between his thumb and first finger to bring it to his lips like it's the first one he's ever smoked. I think it's one of Marv's. Smith is sort of dancing, just working his hips and shoulders.

Wendy comes back and wipes her brow. "Whew," she says to me. "Want to get some air?"

"Sure." I pat Smith on the shoulder and say, "I'll be back in a bit."

I mean, she's in college.

The faggy guy at the door nods to Wendy and says, "*Mon chéri.*" She grins and shakes her head slowly. "Jerry. Too sweet."

It's cold enough to see your breath as we step out toward the cars. Takes a minute for my eyes to adjust, and we almost bump into a couple of guys sitting between cars smoking a joint.

"Sorry," I say.

She stops after a few more steps and leans against an old Toyota. "This is Steven's car," she says.

"Oh."

"God, I'm so glad he finally got here. Those two have been eyeing each other all semester, and Steven was just so scared to come out here."

"Who?"

"Marv and Steven. Like you couldn't tell?"

"Well, uh . . . I was wondering. But why here? I mean, it's a pretty tough crowd."

She looks at me like I'm from Jupiter or something. "Are you . . . blind?"

I laugh. "No. What do you mean?"

"This is the secret jock place. Denny didn't clue you in?"

"No. He just said it was mostly a college hangout. I mean, is *everybody* gay in there?"

"Not everybody. But look around. There are about six women in the whole place. I only came so Steven wouldn't wimp out." She looks me over for a few seconds. "So. . . . You're not?"

"What?"

She gives me a look.

"No," I say. "No."

She nods. We're quiet for a minute, listening to the rhythm from the barn. She changes the subject. "So, you know where you're going next year?"

"You mean school?"

"Yeah."

"Well, Sturbridge. I'm only a junior."

"Oh." She smiles. "So I'd not only be betraying Denny, I'd be robbing the cradle, too."

"What? Oh . . . I guess."

She's not my type. Well, considering the alternative, she definitely is.

"Don't worry," she says. "We'll just hang out. I'll protect you from the boys," she adds with a laugh. "You all right?"

"Yeah."

"Come on," she says. "Let's get another beer. I don't want to miss Marv's next performance."

"Sure. Hey, Wendy?"

"Yeah?"

"Why did Denny . . ."

"Invite you here? You tell me."

I laugh a little, roll my eyes. A van pulls onto the grass and bounces to a stop. Six people get out, two of them girls a bit older than me.

"Dorrie!" Wendy says, and they look over.

"Guys from the U," she says to me. "Straight. We can hang with them if you want."

"Whatever."

She talks to them as we walk toward the barn, and I follow behind. Kevin and Tony and those other dudes would beat the shit out of me if they ever found out about this one.

The guy at the door greets them and pecks the girls on the cheek. He gives me a quick little nod and I go in and look for Smith. He's talking to a couple of guys.

"Hey," he says. "Ronny, you remember Adrian? Ran for Saint Peter's in Wilkes-Barre a few years ago?"

"Hi," I say, shaking his hand, wondering if he's gay and figuring he probably is. He's probably thinking the same about me. Big arm muscles.

"Ron's the one who kicked my ass today," Denny says. Somehow that word "ass" makes me uncomfortable. I look around to make sure no one's checking me out.

"So," I say to Adrian. "Where are you now?"

"Bucknell. This is Joe."

Joe has short bleached-blond hair and is wearing a gray T-shirt that says RUTGERS LACROSSE.

The music gets loud again and somebody starts singing "The Dance," which is another Garth Brooks song I never paid much attention to. Denny's watching the singer—most everybody is turned toward the stage—and I watch Denny from the corner of my eye. He's a confident guy. Seems to know who he is. One of the best runners in the state. I guess that means I am, too.

Wendy asks me to dance when "I Will Survive" comes on, and I shrug and say sure. It's late now; the crowd has loosened up and guys are dancing together. Even Marv and Steven are on the floor, farther apart than the other couples, though, more tentative. Wendy bumps her butt against me and laughs, swirling her arms with the rhythm.

When the song ends she takes my hand and starts rushing toward the front. Marv's pulling Steven along, too. Marv and Wendy grab the microphones. Denny is pushing through the crowd toward us. Marv turns to us and says, "You guys are just backups. You know the song. Meat Loaf. Everybody knows it."

The crowd is nuts. It *is* a rush being up there, even though I'm as much a spectator as a performer. We just shout along with the chorus like everybody else in the barn. Nine-minute song; Marv is sweating like a pig. "Though it's cold and lonely in the deep dark night, I can see paradise by the dashboard light."

We dance another half hour, then get ready to leave. Wendy takes my arm and we step into the night. "I'm heading back to Weston in Denny's truck," she says. "Steven is occupied."

So we get in the truck three across with Wendy in the middle and bump across the field to the road. Smith tunes in the oldies station out of Scranton and rolls down his window. It's cool and a breeze is blowing through the cab.

"Good time?" he asks.

"Great," Wendy says.

"Yeah. Lot of fun," I say. It was.

Denny kind of drums on the steering wheel for a few seconds, probably wondering if I'd ever go back. He doesn't glance my way.

"Lot of fun," I say again. Then we're quiet for a while.

They drop me by the Turkey Hill store. It's still open, but none of my friends are around.

"Thanks," I say. "I guess I'll see you at the districts."

"Better train your butt off," Denny says. "You won't get me twice."

"We'll see," I say, but I know where I stand with him competitively. We're on even ground now—whoever wants it more will take it.

Wendy gives me sort of a one-armed hug and I lean over and shake Denny's hand. "See you guys around," I tell them, and I get out of the truck and run toward home.

What It All Goes Back To

My father let me drive his car to the game, so I'm tuned to one of the town's two FM stations. They're playing "Sister Golden Hair" by America, which I guess was sort of cool several decades ago but isn't exactly what I feel like hearing.

I push the button for the instant shift to the other station, which is playing, I swear to God, "Ventura Highway" by the same band. That's how hip we are around here.

I park at the elementary school and look for a group of guys acting like a team, since I don't know everyone; most of them are my brother's age. Looks like there are four or five of them shooting around on the upper court.

I pass through the chain-link gate. There's a couple of wallets on the black asphalt, keys, a can of Skoal, and a cell phone. "You Ollie?" I say to one of the guys, a quick-looking guard with spiky red hair.

"Yeah," he says. "You Devin's little brother?"

"Yep." He sends me a bounce pass. I take a long jumper that misses everything and say, "Shit."

Guys nod, stick out their hands. "J.D." "Shifty." Tony Hatcher I know. He puts his hand on my shoulder and says,

"Ron, my man. Good to see you." He asks about my brother, who he was tight with for a while back when they were nothing but trouble. "Tell your mom I said hello," he goes. The tattoo on his bicep says GUTS. His T-shirt says STURBRIDGE WRESTLING.

Red-haired Ollie is saying something about making big bucks this summer, cutting grass over at the state park.

"I applied for that job," says J.D., who's got one little hoop earring and slightly crossed eyes. "I didn't even get an interview. They got something against me over there. Ever since me and my friends got drunk and trashed a picnic area." He shakes his head. "That was like *two years* ago."

My friend Aaron comes walking up, grinning. He's the only guy on the team who's my age. Curtis Wheat is with him. "Got the big man," he says, pointing at Curtis with his thumb.

Curtis is a muscle-bound Irish guy who used to have long black hair, but he shaved it off about four days ago, so it's about a sixteenth of an inch long. You wonder why he would take a chance playing in a ragged-ass summer league like this one. They say he'll be starting at cornerback for Syracuse in the fall. Can't imagine his college coaches would want him risking an injury here. His T-shirt says CITRUS BOWL CHAMPIONS.

Seems like everybody's got scruffy facial hair this summer. Balls keep clanking off the rim. The nets are ripped and hanging. Curtis dunks a couple of times. He's a tremendous athlete. One of the best ever at our high school.

We're playing the team from Pete's Market. Several of them played basketball for the high school a while back.

Referee Butch Landers, who's my shop teacher and the assistant high school coach, blows his whistle. Game time.

Me and the other guards look at each other. "Go ahead," somebody says. So I take the court.

Already there's a holdup. Landers is telling J.D. to take out his earring.

"I just got this pierced today," J.D. says.

"Not my problem," Landers says. "You can't keep that in."

J.D. is pissed.

"Can't he put tape over it?" I ask.

Landers shakes his head. His hair is slicked back, and though he's lean, he's got the size of a former defensive tackle. "We play Pennsylvania high school rules in this league," he says.

J.D. goes over to the sideline and another guy comes on.

"This is bullshit," J.D. says loudly as he struggles with the earring.

"And that's a T," Landers says. "You watch your mouth."

"Dick."

"You want another one?"

J.D. just scowls and looks away. He's our biggest guy other than Curtis. Square-shouldered and strong. Played at Weston South, a big rival. Aaron's cousin.

We fall behind early. Not a surprise, since we haven't ever played together. The other team is guys in their early twenties; several of them played for Landers. That's not a huge credential around here, though. The better athletes rarely even go out for the high school team. Aaron switched over to wrestling last winter after two years of junior varsity basketball. And Curtis didn't play high school hoops at all, though he clearly would have helped them.

The other team maintains a seven- or eight-point lead through the first half, and Landers calls a bunch of fouls on Curtis and J.D., which they argue. It's a physical game, especially inside. We have eight players, and seven of us consider ourselves guards. J.D. played a season at guard for Lackawanna JC and never passes up a chance to shoot, but he moves inside on defense for us. He's a constant target for elbows and hands, having beaten these guys regularly back in high school.

"Son of a bitch is giving them every call," J.D. says at the half.

"Just start running on them," says Ollie, who hasn't stopped running all game. "They're starting to wheeze."

It's true that the fitness level is in our favor. Though you see a lot of the other team's players in the weight room at the Y, it doesn't look like they've done much running. J.D. and Curtis are in shape, and Ollie plays Division III ball at Addison College up in Boston. The rest of us can play all day, if not particularly well. Me and Shifty and Ollie have no upper-body bulk at all.

They've got shooters, and they open the second half with a couple of threes, so we're down by thirteen. I play under the basket for a few minutes as we go with a small but quick lineup. There's shoving and cursing but nothing I'd consider blatant. J.D. and their biggest guy stand nose to nose for a second after a shot goes out of bounds, but all I hear is "Yeah?"

"Yeah."

The upper and lower courts are side by side, separated only by the fence, so a whistle in one game sometimes causes a disruption in the other. Their big man goes up hard off an inbounds pass and Curtis gets a hand on the ball. Whistle blows, Curtis stops. The guy grabs the ball and makes a soft, easy layup. Curtis looks around. "What the hell?"

Landers just shrugs. "Not my whistle," he says. "Pay attention."

We finally get in a bit of a flow, figuring out each other's game, getting the ball inside. We cut the lead to eight, then four. Time's running out when J.D. drives hard, has the ball stripped, and lands on his butt. They get a quick outlet pass and have a scrawny guard way ahead of everybody on a fast break. He brings it to the hoop, taking at least one extra step, and lays it in.

"Nice walk," says Aaron, who's trailing the play.

"Aw," the guy says. "Are those real tears?"

"Screw you," Aaron says. "Take a cigarette break."

Down the other end J.D. and the big guy are pushing each other under the basket. "You want a piece of me?" J.D. says, and the guy throws a punch that lands with a thud on J.D.'s chest. They're on the ground now, and this is right in front of the other team's subs. Suddenly there's six Pete's Market players on top of J.D., kicking the shit out of him. It lasts about three seconds as everybody on the court runs over and starts pulling people away. Landers is blowing his whistle in short little spurts, and the refs from the other game come running up.

Landers looks frantic, waving his arms and yelling, "Cut the crap!" He orders the two teams to go to opposite baskets and stands at midcourt conferring with the other referees. Finally he calls over Aaron and the Pete's Market captain. Then he calls J.D. and the other guy involved in the fight.

He throws J.D. out of the game and gives him a two-game suspension. Same for the other guy.

"That's bullshit!" Curtis yells over to Landers. "What about the rest of their team?"

One of the other refs walks over. "Calm down," he says.

"That sucker's giving his players every call," Curtis says. "What about those other guys who jumped in? What's this bullshit with their whole team piling on one man?"

"I don't like your language," the ref says.

"Okay," Curt says. "It's bull*crap*, okay? Same thing."

J.D. and Hatcher take Curtis by the arm and tell him to forget it. "It was my fault," J.D. keeps saying.

"No it wasn't," Aaron says. "Landers is an asshole. His boys got every call."

J.D.'s got patches of skin missing from his knuckles and under one eye, but he says he's all right. There's like a minute left and we're down by six. Landers is still at midcourt. "Watch your mouths or I'll kick out some more of you," he says in our direction.

Shifty is standing next to me, muttering, "Frickin' Landers. Goddamn alcoholic scumbag." Shifty also goes to Syracuse, where he's studying communications. Ollie is just shaking his head, trying to hold back a smile.

Landers waves his arms in a crossing motion. "Game is over. The score stands." So we lose.

We stand around, joke a little, pick up our wallets and shirts. Tony Hatcher grabs my arm and talks under his breath. "Can you believe these guys care that much about *this?*"

"I know," I say. "Get a life."

"Like it's the NBA finals or something."

Suddenly Landers is yelling again, saying Curt's got a one-game suspension. We all look around, wondering why, thinking Curtis is over here with us. But then we see him across the court, right in Landers's face, giving him more shit. Landers has the ball under his arm, listening to Curtis but not backing up. He finally puts up his hand. "Curt," he says firmly, "walk away or you're out of this league." Curtis walks away. Out the gate. Nobody on the other team would mess with him.

vious lack of respect for the coaching staff. I knew
...ess, but I thought it was mostly unsaid.

...ggest mark of honor in this league, I'm starting to see,
...ave played for the high school team, but to come back
...t the asses of those who did, even years later. Some peo-
...'t grow up much. When I play in pickup games on Sun-
...ornings at the Y, the fights are at least as likely to include
...octors and lawyers and teachers as the plumbers and car-
...ers and road workers.

We have a spectator tonight, a girl with short bleached hair.
...can't tell who she's with. She's kind of quiet but is maybe
wenty and is wearing a Hard Rock Cafe T-shirt.

Pete's Market played the game before ours, and a few of
them wished us luck as they walked off. Their fighter is gone for
he summer. Took a job in Florida.

Curtis and J.D. (without his earring) both show up to watch
the game, but Aaron's gone off to football camp. So we've got
five eligible players: four small guards and Hatcher, who's got a
wrestler's body, not a basketball player's.

We'll run. Pressure the ball. These guys are older than the
last team. Two big black guys who are pushing forty and some
scruffy white guys in their twenties. They show up late, about
two minutes before we could have called a forfeit. We would
have waited, though. They had to come down from Callicoon,
New York, a good half hour away. They're sponsored by Roto-
Rooter of Sullivan County.

Turns out they're in good shape, too. They kick our butts in
the first half. We rush our shots, get no rebounds. We decide at
the half to abandon the zone and go man-to-man. Curtis says we
should press full-court, but Ollie says no, they've got too many
ball handlers.

We mill around for a few minutes. The guys from Pete's
Market are laughing. They had a few spectators, some girls and
other guys their age.

The teams for the next game come onto the court and start
shooting. Stan DelCalzo—who is Aaron's father, J.D.'s uncle,
and my former Little League coach—is talking to J.D. Then
Aaron, Mr. DelCalzo, me, and J.D. start walking off. J.D. says
again to us that he's sorry. He goes over to Landers, apologizes,
says he just got off to a bad start with that earring thing. Landers
tells him again that it's not his rule. "We're trying to develop
some of the high school players in this league, so we play by
those rules."

"Yeah? Those guys ain't in high school," J.D. says, waving in
the general direction of the other team. "You let your boys get
away with shit all night."

"Come here," Landers says. He puts his hands on J.D.'s
shoulders. "Let's talk. You and me."

"You've always had it in for me."

Landers gives him a look like What, are you kidding me? "I
don't even know you, pal." Which can't be true, since J.D.
played against Sturbridge twice a year for three years in high
school and was the leading scorer in the conference.

J.D. just looks away as Landers keeps talking, the way he
talks to guys who screw around in shop. Controlling his little
kingdom.

Back under the basket, Mr. DelCalzo is telling me that this
all goes back to junior high school, when J.D. started getting a
reputation in football and basketball, started a long tradition of
Weston South teams beating up on Sturbridge.

A couple of girls call J.D. an asshole as we walk toward the cars. He looks over at the crowd and meets eyes with the guy he fought and says, "Where you gonna be?"

The guy answers, but I don't hear him. J.D. and Aaron get into Aaron's pickup truck and start backing out. Mr. DelCalzo stops them. "Make sure you go straight to the house," he says to Aaron.

Aaron nods.

"Hey," Mr. DelCalzo says.

"What?"

"Aunt Joanie's there," he says, shaking his head, meaning She better not hear a word of this.

That may be the last we see of J.D. this summer. You actually have to show up at a game for it to count toward the suspension, and I'd be surprised if he drove twenty minutes, twice, to watch our team in a league like this. Curtis I can see, since he's local and he's only got to sit out one.

I walk back to the court to get my water bottle. Tony Hatcher's still up there, laughing with some guys from the other team. He comes over to me and says something about some jerks from Sturbridge jumping a Weston player on the street a couple of years ago when it was just the guy and his girlfriend. "The guy was a friend of J.D.'s, so he's had a bad attitude about Sturbridge guys ever since then. It all goes back to that."

Like me, Aaron's just finished his junior year at Sturbridge High School, but he's the one who pulled this team together. Aaron works the front desk at the Y a couple of nights a week, so I played pickup games with him over the winter. Plus we're on the track team together. The other guys he knows mostly from the weight room, and he figured he could build a team around his cousin.

"I felt bad for J.D.," he says to m[e] McDonald's the next night. "He's not h[...]

"He was getting yanked around pretty [...]

"Yeah. But when two guys start fighting [...] says. "You can't have nine guys jumping in on [...]

Aaron's a good running back and a sprinte[r ...] miss our next several games—he's leaving Saturda[y ...] cuse University high school football camp, then c[omes ...] for a day or two before leaving for one at Penn State. [...] badly to play for Syracuse like Curtis, who he's idolized [...] Curtis has our high school sprint records and was the st[ar run]ning back before Aaron.

Aaron is solid but short, and clumsier than you'd expect [on] the basketball court. He always seems to be ready to laugh, eve[n] when he's talking about something serious. "I couldn't believ[e] Curt last night," he says. "He was *mad*."

"Yeah. I'm surprised he's even playing."

"He hates Landers. All the coaches. That's why he wouldn't play basketball for them. He wants to show them up in this league. Oh, man."

"You're not too fond of them either, huh?"

He shakes his head. "Man. Ever since Landers started his son over me on the JV team. It all goes back to that."

The most surprising thing about our first game was how ready these guys seemed to be to fight at the slightest push. They all have dislikes based on actual grievances or simply where somebody went to school or even when, since most of them went to Sturbridge. Several of the better players didn't even play high school varsity, including Ollie, who now starts for an admittedly weak small-college team. There are tons of grudges and an

"At least trap the first pass," Curtis says. "Catch them off guard."

It works once, but Ollie's right. I get stuck guarding one of their big men, but they don't take advantage of it the way they ought to. He keeps posting up on me, but they don't get him the ball. J.D. is yelling from the sideline for guys to drop down and help me out.

The only hint of an incident in this game comes as Ollie is bringing up the ball fast with one of their guys riding him close. Ollie throws an elbow and says, "Get off me, man," and his forehead flushes as red as his hair, but it doesn't develop into anything.

We lose by twenty-two.

"Wish I'd been in there," J.D. says as we huddle up. "That's the type of team I like playing against. Good players, nice guys."

I've gotta give him credit just for showing up. We walk off together and he checks his car carefully, kind of expecting Pete's Market to have scratched it up or kicked in a headlight.

"They do anything?" I ask.

"Doesn't look like it," he says. "Most of those guys are decent, I guess."

I go to the Y three mornings a week after I run—mostly dips and pull-ups and some leg work. It's quiet in there that time of day— a couple of regulars, a few women with a preschooler or two, and Augie. Augie's a retired New York City cop who works part-time in the weight room. Knows everything about everybody who works out here. We talk about food and the Yankees. He keeps talking while you're doing crunches, but I don't mind.

I tell him I took a good shot in the jaw last night trying to block a shot. Tasted blood.

"You'd know it if it was broken, Ron," he says.

"Yeah, I know."

"You guys win?"

"Nah. We don't have it together at all yet."

"How's Tony Hatcher doing?" he asks.

"Good," I say. "Nice guy."

"Yeah. Now he is. He's come a *long* way, though. I seen him down here last week, but I guess he's working a lot of hours now."

"Yeah. He's doing drywall, I think."

Augie is in great shape for somebody in his sixties. He works out like three hours a day. It used to be just weights, but now his doctor has him on the treadmill an hour a day because of a cardiac scare last winter. I'm sure he knows about Hatcher. The kid was a wrestling star a few years ago, then just totally went to hell after his senior season. Got a new set of friends (including my brother, Devin), started using drugs and causing all kinds of trouble. Spent most of that summer in rehab for drugs and alcohol and blew his chance at a college scholarship. He finally started going to Weston Community College this spring and says he's straight, not even cigarettes.

"I'll tell ya," Augie says, "that son of a bitch once, when he was messed up back in high school, I was in the locker room here about to take a shower and Hatcher and this other little shitface, that Corso kid, what's his name . . . Anyway, I go in the bathroom for like two minutes, then I come back to the shower and there's this big pile of piss on the tiles. Hatcher and this Corso kid—Ernie Corso, that's his name; football player—they're out by the lockers and they're laughing their asses off. I go out there and I say to them, I say, 'You little bastards, what the hell is this?' They're like, "What?" And I say, 'You know what. What the hell is wrong with you?' I'm angry now, see? I say, 'This is your Y, too. You do stuff like that in your house?'

"So this Corso kid says, 'What are you gonna do about it? Hit me? Come on.' I'm like, 'No, I'm not gonna hit you. I'm not frickin' stupid. But you clean that piss up or that'll be the end of your membership.'

"Corso starts mouthing off and Hatcher leaves the locker room. Then he comes back with a couple of rolls of toilet paper and starts mopping up the piss. Corso just walks out. I don't think he's ever been back. But I'm like Hatcher's best buddy ever since then. You know, he went into rehab right after that."

"Sometimes we all just need a kick in the ass," I say.

"Oh yeah," Augie says. "We all been there. He's a good kid. Smart. I mean, his father's a frickin' *doctor*, for God's sake."

Our third game is against Shorty's Tavern, which won this league a couple of years ago but has slipped a bit since then. They're local guys, carpet layers and factory workers, mostly in their mid-twenties, slowly getting in worse condition and need-ing knee braces and more tape.

Our T-shirts have finally arrived, dark blue with DELCALZO ELECTRIC in white. Curtis's suspension is over, which should make a big difference inside. His hair is now about an eighth of an inch long. He says he wants it to be long enough to carve his initials into when he gets back to Syracuse.

We jump to a quick lead, Ollie hitting a couple of three-pointers and Curtis and Hatcher getting some put-backs. Ollie is like a coach on the floor, telling me to pressure the point or back off, calling out screens, saying, "I've got two over here" when the zone collapses. He's not the type who'd ever tell me I suck, but after I miss a long shot when he was open inside he says, "You gotta see me in there, Ron" as we run back.

Ollie goes nonstop, lifting the rest of us, and our lead is double figures by halftime.

Second half I'm standing on the sideline with Curtis and J.D., watching Shorty's chip away at our lead. Ollie has the ball at the top of the key and starts to drive. "Take it to the closet!" Shifty yells.

I give him a quizzical look. Shifty laughs. "We call him the closet masturbator." The thin girl with bleached hair laughs, too. Maybe she's here to see Ollie. Tonight she's wearing a shirt that says FORT LAUDERDALE. She brought two gallons of water for us and some paper cups.

The ball gets slapped away by their head-shaved point guard, and Shorty's goes on a rare fast break. Ollie fouls the guy on the layup and he goes to the line with a chance to cut the lead to six.

"Bad call," says Curtis, who's kept his temper in check despite the fact that Landers is refereeing again. Curtis told me before the game that he'd wanted to beat the shit out of Landers last week but just barely held back. He wasn't sure why.

They continue to wear us down, getting the ball inside, and our shooting goes cold. We're up a point in the final minute and they've got the ball.

The shaved-head guy's been quiet all night, but he takes over now. He dishes it inside, they kick it back out, and he nails a three. They pressure the inbounds pass and Ollie makes a rare mistake, throwing it away. They play keep-away for thirty seconds until we have to foul. They hit both ends of the one-and-one, and we're down by four.

Ollie dribbles up in a hurry, shoots a long three, and incredibly gets fouled on the all-time stupid defensive play. But the shot rolls out. He hits two free throws, misses the third on purpose, and they get the rebound as time runs out.

Saturday Aaron's back at the Y, the only day he's home between camps. He says he did well up at Syracuse, got some attention from the coaches, ran a 4.4 forty.

"Yeah," he says, "but don't say nothing about this, but I got bad news about Curt."

"What?"

"He flunked out."

"Shit. Really?"

"Yeah. The coaches said he never came in for help or anything about getting into summer classes or nothing."

"That sucks."

"Yeah. Don't say anything, okay?"

"I wouldn't. Can he get back in later?"

"Doesn't look like it." He shakes his head. "Man, he's *smart*, too."

Thunderstorms roll in late Monday afternoon, so the games are moved up to the high school gym. I get there early and sit on the floor against the bleachers with Ollie and Shifty, watching Roto-Rooter blow out Pete's Market.

Shifty's in his standard game outfit—baggy team shirt with the sleeves ripped off, knee-length shorts, and a tight necklace that looks like BBs strung on a wire. He's the scrawniest guy on the team; never works out except a bit of basketball. I ask him if he hangs out with Curtis up at Syracuse, fishing around to see if he knows anything about Curt dropping out.

"Not much last year, with his football schedule and

everything, but we're rooming together this fall. We found an apartment off campus. Should be great."

Landers is refereeing the game. "Did you play for him?" I ask.

"Just freshman football," Shifty says.

"I played JV for him for a year," Ollie says. "He'd put me in with like thirty seconds left, behind by forty points, and say, 'I want you to make something happen.' Like, come *on*. He wouldn't let us pressure the ball anyway. I couldn't stand it."

One of Pete's players, a very tall thin guy with a ponytail who didn't play in the game against us, misses a layup, gets the rebound, and misses again.

"That's one of Landers's boys there," Ollie says.

"Who is it?"

"Darren Brogan."

"Oh." I remember him now. "Didn't recognize him."

"Two years and a lot of drugs," Shifty says.

It's very humid in the gym and we're sweating heavily just sitting there. I can't even get the tape to stick to my ankles. We play the Sturbridge Building Products team tonight. They're huge but slow, the oldest team in the league on average, and the heat's going to be a problem for them. We start wondering why we're the only three players from either team in the gym.

"Shit!" Ollie says. "We must be playing at the middle school."

We get up and see that the rain is coming down in torrents, but we race out the door and run the two hundred yards to the other school. Most of our guys are in there warming up. We go to the locker room to dry off with paper towels.

J.D.'s back tonight, but Curtis doesn't show. Mr. DelCalzo is there to watch. He looks almost too young to have a kid who's almost eighteen. He tells me Aaron roomed with the nephew of one of the Syracuse coaches at camp and they hit it off real well. "Aaron's gotta get his SATs up," Stan says, "but he could play there."

The blond girl's name is Jess. We get to talking a little. Says she met Hatcher at a Narcotics Anonymous meeting last spring. They've been hanging out on and off ever since. "He helped me through a lot of painful things," she says. So I guess she isn't with Ollie after all.

The game follows a predictable pattern. We fall behind early, make a run, fall behind again, then get frantic. J.D. finds his range in the second half and starts hitting long three-pointers, and Hatcher plays his best game inside, just outhustling everybody for rebounds. The Building Products players are struggling with the heat, so we substitute freely and run them off the court.

They were undefeated, we were winless. But we should be 3–1 by now instead of 1–3.

Tony Hatcher was the top-ranked wrestler in all of Pennsylvania at 140 pounds for most of his senior season. He went to the state meet as the number one seed but got caught in a cradle in the first period of his first match by a kid from out in Altoona. Tony worked his way through the wrestle-backs and finished fifth, sitting in the bleachers for the championship round as his teammates won titles at 130 and 135.

Things started declining, or at least the decline became apparent, when he got in a shouting match with his coach on the van ride back from Hershey, a ride that should have been celebratory. Tony went on a long, wild drunk beginning five minutes after the van left him off at the high school.

He quickly turned away from Al and Digit—the state

champions—guys he'd been inseparable from for at least six years. He still had scholarship offers from Rutgers and Bloomsburg, but a few other schools that had been showing interest pulled out.

Graduation was just a few months off, and unlike my brother, he managed to slide on through. But by the time summer came he was into cocaine and Jack Daniels and Marlboros.

"It wasn't just the wrestling," he told me the other day. "Not blowing it in the states, anyway. It was a long time coming. My father never shut up about my future, not as long as I can remember, and the coach ran the team like a drill sergeant. It was like I wasn't even accomplishing these things on my own, or for me. I just said screw it all."

So it was his idea to go into construction, his idea to enroll at Weston CC, his idea that he would try out for the college's basketball team this October despite never having played in an organized league before this one.

"I can't wrestle again," he says. "It's been too long. But I love basketball. I love it even if I ain't any good at it yet."

It is the nature of a summer league that guys have to work, or they go to the Jersey shore for a few days, or they just plain don't feel like showing up. This is our fifth game and we haven't fielded the same lineup yet. Curtis doesn't show again.

The humidity's finally broken and there's no chance of rain. Mr. DelCalzo shakes his head when I ask him if he's seen Curtis. "Not lately, Ron," he says. "You heard what happened?"

"Yeah. Aaron told me."

"Apparently he was always in trouble with the coaches," Stan says. "Mouthing off in practice and shit. He just goes into these rages. I don't get it."

Shifty has wandered over, shirt hanging out, BB beads around his neck. "You talking about Curt?" he asks.

"Yeah."

"I left him like six messages last week," Shifty says. "He finally left me a message that he had to go back to Syracuse early. Some kind of preseason conditioning program for the defensive backs."

"In June?" Mr. DelCalzo asks.

"That's what he said." Shifty looks out at the court for a minute, then grins and shakes his head.

"You buy that?" I ask.

"I don't know." He shrugs. "Not really. I think he went to his father's place down in Philly."

"*Big* mistake," Mr. DelCalzo says. "You didn't hear what happened? With school?"

"I kind of figured it out," Shifty finally says. "Guess I'm screwed. He owes me three hundred bucks for the deposit on the apartment."

Only five of us show up. Aaron's still at Penn State, so it's me and Shifty and Ollie in the backcourt, Hatcher and J.D. up front. Mr. DelCalzo has Aaron's shirt with him and says he'll go in if we get in foul trouble.

The team we're playing is basically last year's varsity team at Wallenpaupack. Butch Landers is officiating.

We play a tight zone, forcing them to shoot from the perimeter. It's a quick game, with more running than any we've played so far. Somehow we seem looser, more fluid, and we get some fast-break points and move the ball around well. The bleached-hair girl is yelling for Hatcher; they were holding hands before the game.

Ollie always brings up the ball, using Shifty and me on the wings, making good passes inside. We talk to each other, crash the boards, and hustle our butts off all night.

That's how it is on a team; five players on the court trying to fit together. It's about knowing who you are. Choosing the right ones to play with or making the best of the group you're thrown in with. Giving yourself a kick in the ass.

Knowing where you end, where the other ones who matter begin.

Dawn

For two days I have been surrounded by lithely writhing dancers, intensely brilliant cellists and singers, and lyrical expressers of inner-city/rural/suburban angst and desire.

You may have heard of the Griffito Conference, a weeklong summer workshop for teenage poets, musicians, and dancers. It's sponsored by some giant corporation like Microsoft or the Republican Party.

I'm being cynical. It's sponsored by the Griffon Foundation, which is apparently a big deal in its own right.

They run contests and auditions in late winter to attract several dozen of us for a week of (this is from the brochure) "sharing, learning, experimentation, and growth in the idyllic setting of the lakeside Athenaeum Institution in western New York State."

I like words. But no way in hell do I belong here.

My English teacher (and track coach) badgered me to apply. He tells me I have a point of view, and I suppose I agree with him. When I write lyrics, which isn't often, I just write about what I'm going through after making a jerk out of myself with a girl or feeling powerless and stupid after an argument with my father. And I don't go comparing myself to a wilted dandelion or using metaphors or that other shit; I just lay out the emotions and try to let you know what I'm saying instead of expecting you to interpret.

But I am way outclassed here. By everybody.

My mother dropped me off in Scranton early Sunday and I boarded a bus for Erie, six hours away. After a two-hour wait I took a second bus to Jamestown, New York, where I was picked up in a van and driven another half hour to the gates of the Institution, arriving dehydrated and nervous at dusk.

"We're so glad you're here, Ronny," said Mrs. Henderson, the gray-haired conference director, when I showed up at the dorm. "You missed dinner. You're in one of the singles—the rooms are tiny, but we hope there'll be as much interaction as possible." She brought her hands together in a sharp little clap, touching her fingertips to her chin. "You must be exhausted. Are you?"

I let my gym bag slip down off my shoulder and grabbed the handles. "I guess I'm okay. Thirsty, maybe."

She smiled. "We have bottles of water, lots of them, in that little room over there. In the fridge. Today we just get to know each other. At dinner, for example."

I started to say something about getting a bottle of water, but she was only taking a microsecond to breathe. She clapped her hands again and said, "Now, you-ou . . . are in room 2-H. It's a little musty. You don't have asthma or anything?"

"No. Not, uh . . . no."

"Then you'll be fine. So glad you're here. The other poets . . . it's a diverse group. Such sweet girls. And Ramon—

he's from the Bahamas. Just four boys in the poetry group. Ten
girls. You're not a smoker?"

"No. I run."

"We ask that you smoke outside. . . . So. You've arrived."
I nodded and pointed toward the stairs. "Up here?"

"Yes." She smiled tightly. "You'll be fine. Just fine."

On Monday morning they brought everyone together for an in-
spirational talk on creativity by some professor from Cornell.
Then the dancers headed off for the dance hall, the musicians
for the conservatory, and the poets stayed put in the dormitory
conference room.

Jim, the guy running the poetry strand, is about thirty, with
short dark hair and glasses. He teaches at Kenyon College. He
read us a few of his poems—dense, self-absorbed, and pomp-
ously literate. Strange, because he's witty and cheerful, the type
who probably plays volleyball at picnics. He was wearing a golf
shirt and expensive sandals; most of us were in T-shirts and
shorts. A few of the girls were in halters.

We did the usual getting-to-know-you exercise, going
around the circle to state our name, place, interests, and hopes
for the week. Ramon likes MTV and women of all types. He
considers himself a lyricist as much as a poet, "but what's the difference anyway? Nassau rocks; you must visit me there," he says.

Sue is Nebraskan and her poems cover "horses, desires, and
eating disorders." Molly is down from Toronto and writes about
"Eclectic Stuff. Rivers. Rage. Ice cream." She giggles.

Dawn. From outside Boston. Stunning to look at. I'd have
placed her in the dance group if I'd had to guess. "Tom Waits.
The Pogues. Irwin Shaw—his stories more than the novels.

Coffee, carrots, blueberries. Nat King Cole. Jack London. Anything by Toni Morrison or Annie Proulx." Her navel is pierced with a silver ring.

Twice back home I've given books to girls I was interested in. Salinger's *Nine Stories* to a smart-mouthed hurdler with nimble legs; *Cannery Row* to a girl I shared a joint with at a party. They both said things like "Wow, this looks great I can't wait to read it" and then never mentioned books, or reading, again.

I'm in the dark when it comes to women. Like anybody else I'm wanting physical release more than anything cerebral. Is it too much to ask for both in the same package? Maybe not. Maybe here.

My turn. I try to be funny. "I'm from this little hick town in Pennsylvania. Mostly I run track and cross-country and play summer-league basketball. I read a lot of stuff. Magazines. A few novels. I gets C's in English. My poems are simple and I've only written a few. I hang with my friends on Main Street and we bust each other's chops about zits and parents and masturbating. I'm a big TV watcher. A slug." I don't mention my batting average with women, which is zero.

They were all looking at me, of course, since I was speaking. But my eyes met Dawn's. She was smiling at me, looking interested. I hope I wasn't blushing.

Mrs. Henderson keeps stressing to us that the Foundation is eager to bring about cross-cultural and cross-discipline understanding, so we should strive to interact as artists, rather than poet to poet or clarinetist to oboe player. So we have assigned tables at dinner, and there are opportunities to bike or play basketball or dance recreationally after hours. Before dinner on

Monday I played two-on-two basketball with Ramon and a couple of ballerinas. My teammate was Christina, who is leggy with short straight hair, big eyes, and plainly beautiful features. Also the high, muscled butt of the well-trained athlete. She sucks at basketball, though.

Ramon is a showman, making elaborate drives and behind-the-back passes that left his teammate, Tanya, in a state of amusement and confusion.

We won, despite Christina, but neither girl seemed to notice how well I shoot jumpers. They were both intrigued by Ramon, who has an endless capacity to coyly suggest having sex without ever really bringing it up. "I *love* to drive the lane," he says after scooting past Christina for a layup. He was talking about swimming in the lake at night as I slipped away after the game.

After showering I went down to the cafeteria. My table included Sue, the Nebraskan poet; an instructor from the music school and two of his students; and Christina. Yes.

Jerry, the instructor, dominated the dinner conversation by telling about his recent trip to Europe. He was interesting and funny, but I'd rather have been flirting with Christina. She did not seem to be flirtatious, so I looked around and spotted Dawn at another table. She was talking to a musician.

I followed Christina out just for the hell of it. "Need to brush my teeth," she said, which I took as a dismissal. "Then maybe a walk by the lake."

"Sounds nice."

"Join me."

My heart began to race. "Uh . . . okay," I said. "I'll meet you right here."

I ran upstairs, brushed my teeth vigorously, gargled with mouthwash, and reapplied deodorant. Then I ran back down.

It was at least twenty minutes before she returned, and she had four other people with her, two of them guys.

We are not the only ones here this week, not at all. The Institution is a gated community that's bigger than the town I live in, and it's all tree-sheltered old homes and small inns and shops. Families come here for a week or a summer of swimming and boating; the symphony plays at night in a wooden amphitheater; there are lectures and classes on chess and philosophy and creative writing and religion. It all seems safe and white and sort of artificial, what with the gates and the wealth and the security patrol on bicycles. The grounds are about a half mile wide and three times that long, and everything slopes toward the water.

The lake was beautiful; the walk was boring. They were all dancers, and the talk was entirely over my head. I said nineteen words in the next ninety minutes and was relieved when we got back to the dorm.

This morning—Tuesday—we read poems we'd been told to bring with us. First a personal favorite from a published work, then one of our own for discussion. I read Gary Soto's "Profile in Rain," then what I think is probably my best, called "The Hour Before." It's about warming up for the state cross-country championships last year, the anguish you go through, afraid you'll fail, the heat building inside you, the growing calm as you focus and remember how hard you worked to get there.

Reading one of my poems in front of a dozen other writers is almost as nerve-inducing as racing.

Some of the other poets are truly amazing. Ramon, for all

his cockiness and flash, reads an introspective poem about the beach at night after his father has left in drunkenness and anger, comparing the reflection of the moon on the water to the way he sees himself in his dad.

Melanie, a quiet girl from New Jersey, cracks us all up with a hilarious poem about getting dressed for a junior high dance.

At lunch, I hesitate on the buffet line, pondering a choice of tuna salad or bologna. I opt for yogurt and several pieces of fruit. You can sit wherever you want to at lunch, so I scan the room for a spot. Then I set my tray on the counter near the juices. As I'm filling a glass with fruit punch I feel a knock against the back of my knee, and I tilt forward slightly and spill it on the counter.

"Hey," Dawn says, grinning at me.

"Hi. Was that you?"

She kind of flicks up her eyebrows. "Mmm-hmm."

"Thanks."

"You're welcome."

What a smile. She again becomes my immediate, intense priority.

"Where are you sitting?" I ask.

"Right there," she says, pointing. "I saved you a spot."

I get a fresh glass of juice, shut my eyes for a second, and say a silent prayer of thanks. Then I join her at the table.

"They're bringing in a DJ tonight," she says.

"Really?"

"Yeah. You can dance, right?"

I roll my eyes. "Some."

"You must have strong legs," she says. "All that running."

"Yeah," I say. "I go fine when I'm moving in a straight line. Dancing is a different matter."

"I love to dance," she says. She beats out a rhythm on the table. "You ever do a poetry slam?"

"You mean like a reading?"

"No. Well, yeah. But a slam is physical, too. Very animated. You get up and perform your poems, like a storyteller. It's where poetry and muscle overlap." She flexes her bicep. There's a tiny star tattooed on her shoulder. "I'm putting together a slam for Friday night. You're up for it, right?"

"Sure," I say, kind of tentative. Then I realize that no one knows me here; I can be anybody I want to be. "Definitely," I say with some authority. "I'll be there."

I squeeze in a workout before dinner, kind of a slow anticipatory run along the lake. No sense tiring out my legs. I think real hard about what to wear tonight, but I don't have many options. Shorts. Running shoes. The adidas T-shirt, I guess. It's clean.

Around nine I start looking for Dawn. I know I'll see her at the dance hall, but I'd like to meet up with her first, let people notice that we arrive together. But I don't find her. So I walk the hundred yards alone.

I see her right away, dancing with a group of girls. Her shirt is low-cut and her skin is glistening. The music is coming from a cheap little boom box, and there's no sign of a DJ. There are only about fifteen people in the room. I take a seat in a wooden folding chair.

After about four songs she comes over to me.

"What's going on?" I say.

"Nothing much," she says. "They said the friggin' DJ isn't going to show. What a rip."

"Yeah."

She gently grabs my arm. "Come on," she says, leading me toward a small stage on the other side of the room. There's a tiny booth there with a chest-high window. She opens a door on the side and we enter the booth.

"I can do this," she says.

There are two CD players, one on either side of the counter in front of the window, with a flat soundboard between them— knobs and lights and a stick for mixing the songs from the two CDs. She turns a couple of switches and leans over the microphone.

"Dawn and Ronny are in the house," she announces. "Brothers and sisters, let's crank it up."

She slips in something by a girl group and turns up the volume, then starts going through the CDs. There's a lot of classical stuff, of course, since this is the ballet hall. But there are about a dozen contemporary rock/dance-mix CDs and some greatest-hits collections: the Stones, Madonna, R.E.M.

"We'll be all right," she says. "We'll rock."

I catch on real fast and work the CD player on the right. You get the track ready to go, then start it just as the left one is finishing. Dawn works the stick and does some smooth transitions. Before long there are at least thirty people dancing.

There's a lot of bumping around in the close quarters of a DJ booth, leaning over to pop out a disk, working the mix stick, reaching for CD cases, an intentional elbow to the bicep. We take turns drinking from a bottle of Sprite; I cap the bottle and shake it between sips, slowly releasing the carbon dioxide to make it flat.

"Quirky," she says.

"Tastes better," I say.

"Whatever."

"I know what I'm doing," I say. I burp too much if it hasn't been defizzed.

I reach in close when I hand the bottle to her. We dance in place. She lights a filtered Camel.

Ramon brings over a predictable CD. Dawn looks at it, pronounces it danceable. He leans into the booth, talking to her, making her laugh. He's smooth, he's polite, but you can tell he's thinking they'll be gittin' jiggy wit it later. Poet, my ass. She gives me a sly smile when he leaves.

There's a certain intimacy in her cigarette smoke, how she doesn't bother to turn her head but lets the barely visible stream envelop me. The pursing of her lips to release the smoke, the touching of her tongue to her teeth. The night goes on. We sip from a bottle of sneaked-in beer. I have to remind myself continually not to stare at that pocket of skin between her breasts, though her outfit is shouting at me to do so. It's saying Look, look closer. Don't even blink; it'll disappear.

The place starts clearing out after midnight, but we go on until one. We straighten up a little, turn off the equipment.

"We rocked," she says. "This is a permanent gig unless the DJ shows tomorrow." She bumps my thigh with her butt. "Let's go."

We head for the dorm and she's giddy and talkative and she puts her hand on my shoulder. We stand outside and laugh a little, teasing, joking about how sanitized the Institution feels. I am drained of energy, but I won't be able to sleep. There is no supervision in the dorm; she could stay in my room. But I'm very patient. I'll wait until tomorrow. I've been waiting all my life.

I brush my teeth, cup water in my hands, and rinse. I pull my shirt over my head and press it against my face. A T-shirt is the best absorber of scents: her smoke, your sweat, and something else entirely, something spicy, something definite and permanent from Dawn. Something tangible to take to bed with me. Almost like sleeping with her.

I have a hard time concentrating during the Wednesday-morning poetry sessions, glancing over at Dawn, thinking about tonight. I blow off lunch and go down to the tiny pharmacy at Bellinger Plaza near the amphitheater for breath mints and condoms.

We break into pairs in the afternoon to try collaborative poems. I'm with Molly, the Canadian. She has developed a hopeless attraction to Julio, a deadpan wit from New Mexico with bushy black hair, three earrings, and large teeth. I confess that I'm hung up on Dawn (but I'm pretty confident about where that's leading). We decide on an ambiguous crush poem, one that could work in any combination of genders.

I let Molly do most of the work. She is self-deprecating and sweet, and aware of the great odds against her. Our group is ten females to four guys; the dance group is even more decidedly feminine. Only the musicians have a more or less equal ratio, so this is a terrific place to be a guy.

I take a long run in late afternoon, stopping to stare at the lake and feel the blood pumping through my muscles. I take a hot, lengthy shower and stay quiet at dinner. I wave to Dawn but stay cool. Then I return to my room to read.

I wait until after nine-thirty to walk to the dance hall, hoping to create anticipation on her part. The place is much fuller tonight; the word must have gotten around. But there's a guy in the DJ booth, and he's older than any of us.

So we won't be in there tonight, but it's just as well. I'd

rather dance with her out here. I'd rather be able to break away early. She looks incredible. Dark halter top, short denim skirt, leather sandals, a choker of Navajo beads.

She finds me right away, touching my wrist. "How was your run?" she asks.

"Great," I say. "Invigorating." I say this suggestively. I can't help it. She is coy enough not to react yet.

"Where've you been?" she asks.

"Hanging out," I say. I jut my chin toward the DJ booth. "The professional showed up, huh?"

She shakes her head in faux disappointment. "Too bad," she says. "We kicked ass."

"Definitely. We should see what else we'd be good at," I say, trying to sound a bit like Ramon.

She nods slowly but stares out at the dancers.

"We should get out there," I say, meaning the dance floor.

"Yeah," she says. "I'll be back."

She walks off toward the bathroom. I notice Molly talking to Julio, laughing on the other side of the room. And Ramon is dancing tight with Tanya, the ballerina he tried to seduce on the basketball court.

Dawn is gone a long time. I stick my head outside and find her smoking on the steps.

"Hey," I say.

"Hey."

"You all right?"

"Yeah. Just needed a smoke." She crushes it in the dirt and gets up to join me. We go in and start dancing. I guess she's okay.

The dancing feels awkward at first, and she's looking

around instead of at me. But she loosens up after a couple of songs, and soon we're laughing and bumping and working up a sweat.

We leave at midnight and head for the lake. The grounds are dark and quiet, and the sky is a mass of stars between the treetops.

"Great night," she says, taking my hand. "Look at the Dipper. It's so huge."

We take a seat on a dock, the water lapping all around us, smelling cool and deep and weedy.

"I could stay here all night," she says, closing her eyes and inhaling.

"Yeah." This seems to be working, so I say, "I'd love to see the crack of dawn," which is so damn clever I can't believe I said it. I guess she didn't hear me.

We're quiet for a few minutes. When she speaks it's just above a whisper. "I try to kill a whole night when I can, just letting it wash over me. Not trying to think or even move much. We forget that there's two sides to the day."

"We can stay up," I say. "We can lie on this dock until dawn comes."

This time she gives me what people refer to as a sidelong glance. There's a slight little twitch at the corner of her mouth while she ponders whether that was Freudian or intentional. That could be a smile starting, so I push it further and say, "Or I do."

The twitch becomes a full-fledged sneer, and she turns away with a single word: "Asshole."

She sits forward now, staring at the lake, then fumbles in her pocket for a cigarette. She smokes it sort of disdainfully, if you can picture that. When the smoke is over, she stands up. "We'd better get back."

My God, I'm a shithead.

Thursday is painful. I don't even remember the sessions. I don't participate except when I'm called on.

I say screw dinner and walk over to Bellinger Plaza, getting a turkey-and-what-looks-like-seaweed sandwich on yuppie bread made of cornhusks and acorn chips. I have no appetite anyway. Needless to say, Dawn avoided me. Needless to say, this entire week has been an embarrassment.

I walk for three hours, making loops around the perimeter of the Institution. When I'm tired enough, I walk past the dance hall, which is not crowded but is still pumping out music.

Tomorrow this will be over. Saturday I'll take two buses. Sunday night I'll be back on Main Street. Monday I'll begin training for the fall.

I am not an artist. Muscle can beat art. Muscle can rip through a painting and shatter a sculpture and splash through a reflection in the moonlight.

Muscle kicks ass. It means something.

Friday in class Molly reads "our" poem aloud:

Unstraightened hair
Pulled back but bushy
Piled high
Glossy
Strands unwinding
Reaching

Dark
Rich and black
Unstraightened
Unreachable
Unrequited
Unreal

The class applauds. We applaud for all the poems.

Dawn says, "Don't forget the slam tonight, everybody. Three minutes apiece before the dance. Tell everybody from the other groups about it."

I feel a little better. Class is over. I walk out alone.

"You coming tonight?" she says from behind me.

I turn. "Sure."

She nods, hesitates, walks back inside. "See you there."

It goes well. Dawn is great. Molly, too. I do two quick poems. I start with "Waiting for You in the Produce Aisle," which I figure will get a laugh.

Jenny, Jenny, Jenny
I would spend a penny
for every second in your arms . . .
not to exceed twenty-five dollars.

That's the whole poem. It gets a decent reaction. I follow it with "The Hour Before." I close my eyes halfway through, stop trying to perform. I just say it, slow and steady, and I feel it again. The way I felt when I wrote it.

I will fail again
If not this time, then another

And the failure will propel me
And I'll triumph once again.

That is a poem that is too personal to share, too preachy and unrefined. But I've given it two audiences this week. Maybe that will help me revise it.

The dance is wild, a release and a celebration for most. I stay to the side, still wounded. Dawn comes up to me later, unraveled and perspiring. She stands there. I stand there. We stand there.

"A bit of advice," she finally says, "since you seem like a decent guy." She's not exactly looking at me, just kind of beyond me toward the dancers. "You could have had me." This is straight talk—no blushed whispering for her. "It would have taken another night or two, and it would have been my choice, not yours. But it would have happened if you'd let it. It would have happened."

The next morning I pack my gym bag and hustle downstairs for my ride into Jamestown. Mrs. Henderson shakes my hand and tells me again how wonderful it was to have me. Ramon is packed and waiting. He shakes my hand, says I must come see him during Carnival.

Dawn is there, too. She comes over and gently smacks my arm.

I nod for a few seconds, thinking what to say. Sorry seems stupid, so I say thanks instead.

"Yeah," she says. "Okay."

"I'm glad I was here," I say. "It's been something."

The van pulls in. I pick up my bag. I look back at Dawn. I move forward.

I'll spend today on buses; I'll spend tomorrow resting. To-morrow night I'll go for a long, long run. Through town. Out of town. In the dark, in the cool, in the night.

I'll run so far that the night will wash over me.

I'll run so far I'll reach daylight.

Thanksgiving

"You need to go get Devin," my father said to me Wednesday morning. "I'm working; your mom's busy. Take the car. You know how to get there."

"There" is Kutztown University, where my brother was a twenty-one-year-old freshman. The big blowup that had been brewing ever since he became a teenager had finally happened midway through his senior year of high school. He left in a hurry, and we barely heard from him for two years. He got arrested a few times, but nothing major. Came home last January, got his GED while working at Kmart, and seemed to be enjoying college.

I had a half day of school, which I could have blown off, but I went anyway and then headed out toward Kutztown after getting a chicken sandwich at McDonald's. The weather was cold but clear, no sign of what was to come.

It's an easy two-hour ride down, mostly on smaller rural highways. I blasted tapes and played out some races in my head and figured I'd be home in time to hang out with Kevin and Tony that night.

Devin's dorm room smelled smoky and he wasn't ready to

go. I sat on his unmade bed while he threw some things in a duffel bag.

"Heard you got like fifth in the state or something?" he said.

"Third, actually." I'd been leading the state cross-country championship with a quarter mile to go but couldn't quite hold on. I'll get 'em in the spring.

He tied his hair in a ponytail and picked up a paperback novel from his desk. He stared at the book a few seconds, then put it and a second one in the duffel bag. Then he asked me to stand up and he reached under his mattress and took out a little Ziploc bag of pot.

"You better drive," he said as we walked across the campus. "I've got a bit of a buzz."

We ran when we reached the parking lot because it had started to rain. We got in and I popped out the tape. It was country music, and I didn't want Devin to see it. But he did.

"What the hell is that?" he said, and he laughed. He fiddled with the radio and found the college station.

I drove out the gate and stopped at a traffic light. "So how's the dick been treating you?" Devin said.

I looked down at my crotch and then looked at him sideways.

"I mean *Dad*," he said. "He busting your chops?"

"He leaves me alone pretty much."

"The last hurrah."

"What do you mean?" I asked.

"He's out of there as soon as you graduate."

"You think?"

"Definitely. They've been counting the days."

Maybe that's true. Maybe not. Devin's been saying I should move down here with him when school gets out, but I don't expect to be going to Kutztown. I've been getting some interest from Division I schools ever since the state meet. The good ones like Northeastern and Pitt back off in a hurry when they hear my grade point average, but my coach is saying I'll get at least a partial ride somewhere.

"Mom making a turkey tomorrow?" he asked.

"Far as I know."

We worked our way out of farm country and through Allentown, and by the time we reached Route 33 it was raining pretty hard and the wind was blowing like a bastard.

"Mom will be better off without him," Devin was saying. "He just brings everything down."

Hard to imagine the house without my father in it, but Devin had a point. There hadn't been a lot of jocularity the past few years. But hell, it's the only family we got.

The wipers weren't great, so I had to scrunch down a bit to see under the streaks. I put the lights on even though it shouldn't have been dark for another hour. Devin had his eyes shut. We'd lost the Kutztown station miles before, so I put in a Beatles tape I'd been listening to a lot. "Good shit," Devin said.

Route 33 ended and the car slid a bit on the on-ramp to Route 80, but I kept it on the road. The streaks on the windshield were turning to ice and the wipers were making sort of a *pick-pock* sound. And then we were sliding worse, the road a sudden sheet of black ice.

"Better brake!" Devin said. "There's something up ahead."

"I *am* braking!" I said. But we weren't stopping. There were cars in the road ahead of us, stopped and turned sideways and smoking.

"Keep the wheel straight," he said, reaching over, but we were starting to spin and we were definitely going to crash.

"Hold on," I said, and things seemed to slow down in my head. And I watched the distance between us and the pileup grow smaller, bracing for the crash, feeling the car move in a sickening shimmy I couldn't stop.

The front passenger side collided sideways into a silver Buick and our car spun around, coming to a stop facing west, the direction we'd just come. "Get out!" Devin said, unbuckling his seat belt and shoving my arm.

"Get out?"

"I can't open my door. Next vehicle hits us head-on. Get out!"

I scrambled out and Devin followed. Seconds later a pickup truck did just what Devin said it would do, and we watched from the shoulder as our father's red Escort got accordioned.

The sleet was pounding our heads. Devin was in a T-shirt. He tried lighting a cigarette but couldn't.

"Holy shit," I said.

"Jesus." Devin grabbed my arm and we started walking along the shoulder, slipping as we went. "You all right?" he asked.

"I think so. Yeah. Are you?"

"Yeah. Look at this shit." At least a dozen cars and pickups were spread out over about sixty yards in front of us, some of them tipped over, all of them crumpled. We could hear sirens in the distance, but no cops or ambulances were on the scene yet. We passed a car lying on its roof, with two guys bent over talking loud to the driver, who was stuck inside. A woman was standing next to her SUV, which was crunched against the barrier that separated the eastbound lanes from the westbound. She was holding a little girl in her arms, and another young girl was standing next to them shivering. The one standing had some cuts on her face and her ear was bleeding, and all three of them were crying.

Devin went over to them. "Everybody all right?" he said.

"I think so," the woman said, kind of trembly. "I couldn't stop. It was so icy."

"I know," Devin said. "Come on. There's an exit up ahead." He took a handkerchief out of his pocket and put it by the girl's bleeding ear. "Hold that there," he said. "Not too tight." He turned to the mother. "Give me the little one," he said. "Come with us."

So Devin carried the smaller girl and the other one took her mother's hand, and we carefully walked the six hundred yards to the exit. "What's your name, honey?" Devin said to the girl in his arms, and she said, "Mandy." "We'll be okay, Mandy. We'll get you warm."

The road was empty ahead of us, of course; nothing could get past that pileup. I walked behind; Devin's strong skinny arms carrying that child, his hair matted to his head and his T-shirt frozen to his skin. I caught up to the woman and said, "We'll be all right," and she nodded and I took the girl's other hand.

There was a gas station/convenience store just off the exit, and the woman called her husband and gave him the story. The clerk gave us some paper towels to wipe off our heads and Devin got a coffee and blew on his fingers. He stripped off his T-shirt and the clerk gave him a Texaco shirt.

An older guy paying for his gas said, "A mess up there, huh?" He told us there was a motel up the road on Main Street in Stroudsburg. We waited a half hour until the husband came by for the mother and daughters, then the guy dropped us off at the motel. He had a heavy pickup, but even that was sliding around.

The lady at the front desk of the Best Western had a blue blazer and a nameplate that said KIM W. She looked up and said, "May I help you?"

"Well," Devin said, "we kind of need a room. We were in that wreck out on Route 80."

"Oh my. You're all right?"

"Yeah."

"You must be frozen."

"We're okay. Do you have any rooms?"

"Yes, of course. Are you sure you're all right?"

"Definitely."

"We don't have much money on us," I said.

"Do you have a credit card?"

Devin shook his head. "No. We could call my dad."

She dialed for us and I took the phone.

"Dad?"

"Yeah."

"Listen," I said. "We were in an accident. A big one."

"Shit. You wreck the car?"

"I think so. There was like fifteen cars involved. We got sandwiched."

"Jesus. Where are you?"

"Um, in Stroudsburg somewhere. We were on 80. It was a sheet of ice all of a sudden. We couldn't stop."

"What'd the cops say?"

"We didn't talk to them."

"Oh, Christ. You just left the car? Where are you calling from?"

"A motel. They need a credit card."

"What the hell for?"

"So we can stay here. We can't go anywhere."

"My ass. I'll drive down and get you."

"Dad, the roads are ridiculous. We should stay put."

"Jesus. . . . Are you guys all right?"

"Yeah, we are."

"Let me talk to Devin."

I smirked at Devin and handed him the phone.

"Hey," Devin said. "Yeah, it's bad. . . . Ronny was. . . . It wouldn't have made any difference. I probably would have got us killed. . . . I don't think so. We were sliding all over the place trying to walk here. . . . We were freezing our asses off. And there were these little girls . . . Screw the cops. . . . By Strouds- burg. . . . You call them. Find out how we can get my stuff. . . . No, it's totaled."

Then he listened for a long time, like a minute. He turned away from me and I heard him sniffle. "I know," he finally said. "You, too. . . ."

"Ma'am," Devin said, speaking to the woman at the desk, "can you talk to my father?"

She took the phone. Devin wiped his eyes and squeezed my shoulder. "Let's ask if they have any toothbrushes," he said.

We got to the room and ordered hamburgers from room ser- vice and hung our socks and pants up to dry in the bathroom. We turned the heat way up and turned on the TV and climbed into the beds. We were both sort of beat, so after the hamburg- ers we nodded off for a couple of hours.

The phone woke us up and we talked to our mom and told her ten times that we were okay. "I'm so grateful," she kept say- ing. "It could have been so much worse. We saw it on the news. Route 80 was closed for three hours."

That evening Devin said we should go out and find a bar. "I'd kill for a beer," he said. "Come on."

The freezing rain had changed over to snow and the plows were out. There was a sports bar right around the corner from the motel, and it was surprisingly crowded. Devin got himself a mug of Rolling Rock—twelve beers on tap, I counted, but most of the guys were drinking bottles of Budweiser or Yuengling—and a glass of Coke for me. There was a band scheduled to play, but I figured no way with the weather.

"Hey," I said as we took a table near the front window.

"What?"

"You think the cops'll look in your duffel bag?"

He scrunched up his mouth and looked at the ceiling. "Nah," he said. "Why would they?"

"I don't know. Maybe they'll smell it."

"It's sealed up. I ain't worried." He should have been. He was still on probation.

Devin lit a cigarette. He was wearing the borrowed shirt—a blue cotton button-down with a Texaco patch on the pocket. He had his hair down, stringy blondish hair parted in the middle and hanging down to his shoulders.

The bar itself was horseshoe shaped and opened into the kitchen. There was a pool table and dartboards in a room off to the side and there was a square smaller bar in there, and the walls were covered with Penn State and Eagles and Penguins memorabilia. Four TVs were on, two of them to a UCLA-Indiana basketball game, one to the NHL, and the fourth, above our heads, to a sumo wrestling tournament.

"You really think they'll get divorced?" I asked.

He stared at his beer for a few seconds, blew out some

smoke. "I don't know," he said. "It doesn't matter, does it? We're both out of there by summer. I'm already gone, aren't I?"

"Yeah, I guess."

He shook his head. "I came back because I missed them, you know? I mean, I always missed Mom. But I even started missing him a little. I wanted something more. You know, so I wouldn't just carry that with me all my life."

He took a swig of beer, draining it. "Wasn't quite what I planned, but I guess I closed the gap a bit. He was okay today once he got over losing the car."

"Yeah," I said. "I suppose you could say that."

Devin smirked, then let out a short laugh. "We had to come close to dying for him to begin to crack, but he did seem relieved that we survived it."

I noticed that two guys were in the corner of the bar with a couple of guitars and some amps, and one of them was testing the microphone. Looked like we'd have entertainment after all.

At least two-thirds of the people in the bar were men, and from the conversations it sounded as if a lot of them had been stranded by the accident, too. Unlike in Sturbridge, about a third of the people were black.

Devin went up to the bar for another beer. "Kitchen open?" he asked.

"Sure," said the bartender, a guy in his twenties with sandy hair combed over a bald spot.

Devin turned to me. "Want wings?"

"Yeah. Definitely."

"Order of wings and a pizza," he said. "Another Coke, too."

The college-age guy with the acoustic guitar up on the little stage tapped the microphone and said, "Hey, out there.

We're . . . well, we would be Bruised, but so far it's just me and the beast from the East, Kenny Oshiro. We should be all right. The others might get here later."

Kenny was a very skinny Asian guy with long black hair and about six harmonicas tucked into his belt. The other guy was short and wearing an ESU Wrestling T-shirt.

"Two, three . . . ," and they started in on a Van Morrison song.

"You *really* think Dad cares about what happened today aside from what it'll do to his insurance payments?" I asked.

Devin laughed. "He said some things after you got off the phone. They'll be down in the morning. Yeah, he was relieved, you know, that nothing really bad happened."

"I guess. You know that he never comes to see me run? I got third place in the whole friggin' state of Pennsylvania and all he said when I got home was 'There's a cord of wood that needs stacking.'"

Devin shook his head, but he smiled a little. "You write poetry and run cross-country, boy. You want Dad's respect, you have to play football and drive a tractor."

I rolled my eyes and smiled. Devin laughed. "He cares. He just never learned how to show it. Cold life growing up on the farm, you know. His father was a prick."

"I've heard."

Kenny Oshiro was doing the harmonica intro of Springsteen's "Thunder Road" and the crowd was starting to take notice. He was good. The other guy had said Kenny was from Japan and just came over a year before "to make it big on MTV."

The pizza arrived and it was huge, plus we had the wings, so we shared some slices with other guys at the bar. Then they bought us a round of drinks and two other band members showed up—the drummer and another guitarist—and the TV basketball game ended and another one came on and more people arrived, including some older couples and a lot of students from East Stroudsburg U.

People learn that you're kids who got stranded on the way home for the holiday and they kind of take you in. We stayed until way after midnight and didn't spend any more money, which was good because we were down to about ten bucks between us. And when we left, the sidewalk was covered in about four inches of fresh white snow and the traffic light at the corner was blinking yellow. Snow was still falling but there was no wind, and I took a good look up and down Main Street, which was almost exactly like the main street in Sturbridge.

"Time to get some sleep," Devin said as we turned toward the motel. "Big day tomorrow. Thanksgiving."

Losing Is Not an Option

Thirty-seven thousand people going nuts at Franklin Field in Philadelphia for the best track-and-field meet in America. Sixteen lean high school kids toeing the line for the 3,200 meters; eight laps of the track. Not just Pennsylvanians in this race: The favorite is from Virginia; a Jamaican kid is expected to challenge; even the Irish guy who anchored the winning distance-medley relay team earlier in the day is trying to double back under brilliant blue skies.

Ron is scared but wired; his mouth feels dry but his armpits and crotch are damp with nervous perspiration. He burps and tastes this morning's Egg McMuffin and shuts his eyes and listens: Caribbean drums in the bleachers and coaches shouting down to the runners; college relay teams packed into the paddock area next to the track, waiting for the race that will follow this one; the deep inhalation of the guy poised to his left, THE ROCK on his purple jersey. The runner to Ron's right is crossing himself; a guy from Quebec trots forward a few yards and bounces up and down, then jogs back to the starting line. The official starter with the yellow sleeve says, "Runners, take your marks." They lean forward and bring back a fist and get ready to pounce at the gun.

This is no dual meet against Scranton.

This is the Penn Relays, and it does not get more exciting than this.

The race is viciously contested, a ridiculously quick 61-second first 400 meters divides the pack in two, with Ron in second place in the second group about six yards behind the leaders. There's elbowing and hands to the back for balance and some spikes to the shins that draw little scratches of blood.

He hangs in there, moves up gradually over the next few laps, and reaches the midpoint in sixth place, a couple of strides off the pace of the kid from Ireland, who takes them through 1,600 meters at 4:25. Ron's lifetime best for 3,200 meters is 9:28, set two weeks ago in winning an invitational down in Allentown; just barely fast enough to get him a call for this race. He'd passed the midpoint at 4:42 in that one.

All week in practice he'd been supremely confident, ripping through 300-meter intervals and ready to step up and kick some butt. Then this morning, the tightening of the stomach with the reality of being here, warming up on the same turf as runners from Villanova, Ohio State, Arizona; the Santa Monica Track Club; the D.C. Striders; NCAA champions—hell, *Olympic* champions; and the high school teams from up and down the East Coast, plus the studs they'd invited in from elsewhere.

Outside the stadium, jogging through the street fair with the cheap jewelry and racks and racks of Penn Relays T-shirts and pretzel vendors and musicians, he'd imagined the race as something like this; survive the torrid early pace, maybe throw in a spurt or two of his own in lap six or seven, winnow it down to a handful of contenders, and hope that his kick would sustain

him. Be this year's unknown who stole a major title. The Penn
Relays history books are filled with such stories.

With two laps to go the Irish runner is struggling, and the kid
from Fairfax, Virginia, moves into the lead. He won the Eastern
regional cross-country title last November and is headed for
Georgetown on a full scholarship, more muscular than anyone in
the field, more a man. The two other Pennsylvanians in the lead
pack are just ahead of Ron—guys from Council Rock and Lancaster Catholic. He knows them well—they'd both burst past
him near the end of last fall's state cross-country championships,
leaving Ron to struggle home in third.

The Virginian extends his lead to five meters while the
three Pennsylvanians pass the Irishman and the bell sounds for
the final lap. Ron sucks it up, sticking with the others. On the
backstretch the Jamaican comes up on his shoulder and darts
past, going wide on the turn in an attempt to move into second.
Every muscle is in play now, every step an agony and every voice
in the stadium at its loudest.

Off the final turn, Ron is fifth but gaining, driving with
everything left in his body. He goes wide to pass them—way out
to lane four, nearly even now with the others, sprinting down
the homestretch, groaning, clawing across the line in 9:11 for
fourth place, less than a second behind the winner.

If he'd been a tiny bit smarter the race would have been
his. An earlier kick; a little more faith in his endurance; a little less memory of that cross-country collapse and he'd have
won it.

Ron was walking up Main Street a few nights after Penn with a
couple of guys, headed toward his old friend Gene's house to

play some poker. They were passing O'Hara's Bar and Grill when a voice called out.

"Hey," Ron said, turning. "Guys, I'll catch up."

Ron's father was in the doorway of the bar. He stepped out and gave his son a clumsy, unexpected hug. "Worked late; I was just getting a hamburger and a beer. Come on in."

Ron's parents had separated just after Christmas, and his father was living with Ron's grandmother in an apartment above a pizza place. Just for a while; just until he figures things out.

"What are you up to?" the father asked, motioning with his head toward a booth in the corner. O'Hara's isn't really much of an after-work bar. More an all-day, linger over a beer and have an occasional shot kind of place. But Ron's father did have a plate of food, and he grabbed it and his beer from the bar and walked over.

"Going to play some cards," Ron answered. "Over at Gene's."

"Been a while since I saw him."

Gene and Ron had been as close as brothers through elementary school, playing stickball and basketball and street hockey and whatever else was in season. Summers they'd play Monopoly or chess to kill the mornings, walk to the community swimming pool, maybe get in a water polo game, then walk to the diner and get french fries. They grew apart when Gene's hormones kicked in about a year ahead of Ron's. Now that Gene is out for track they've found some new common ground.

"So," Ron said, "how you doin', Dad?"

"Pretty good," he said. "Not too bad." He looked at his kid and nodded a bit, the slightest smile on his lips. He was balding and going soft in the face, but he was still the person Ron saw when looking through his father's high school yearbook, the tall gawky defensive end and first baseman on the sports pages. "Mad Stork" to his teammates.

"You want something?" Dad asked. "A soda?"

"Not really. I'm holding up the game, actually."

"Yeah. It's good to see you, though. Come by."

"I will," Ron said. "I told Grandma I'd be by for dinner on Friday."

"Great. I'll be sure to get home on time." He reached over and grabbed Ron's shoulder. "I read about that race in Philadelphia. Close one, huh?"

"Real close," Ron said, frowning a bit. "So friggin' close I don't know how I didn't win it."

Thursday Ron was cooling down after a hard set of 600-meter intervals, jogging on the backstretch in the second lane. It had hurt; it hurt good. He knew he had to make that pain a part of himself, to welcome it, to thrive on it, to insure that when he went for it all at the state championship, when he unleashed that final kick, there would be more than enough to get him to the finish.

"Beep, beep," came a tense but friendly voice. Ron looked back and shuffled into lane three as Darby O'Neill and Ellie Jacobsen came flying past, leading a pack of girls and a few freshman boys. Ellie is tall and dark and angular; Darby is compact and has a long braided ponytail flopping on her neck. Very different runners, very similar results. Both juniors. Two of the best in the area at 400 and 800 meters.

Darby glanced back and smirked at Ron. "I'll run you down, man."

He laughed. "Not hardly."

Ron stopped at the turn and gently stretched, reaching for the track, palms flat, hair hanging into his eyes. He held that position, feeling the pull in his hamstrings, then sat down in lane five and did a set of sixteen crunches followed by sixteen push-ups.

By then Darby was approaching again, taking it hard on the final interval of the day. Ron stood and watched her, twenty yards ahead of Ellie, efficiently pumping her arms. "Looking good," he said.

"Push me," she answered, puffing out the words. So he followed her on the turn, taking the second lane and saying, "Work it, Darby. All the way."

And he pulled even at the head of the straightaway and eased into a kick, hearing her *ehh, ehh, ehh* as she worked to hold him off.

He matched strides with her, not straining and not moving ahead, just opening up and stretching it out and giving her a pace to hold on to.

"Thanks," she said as she stumbled to a stop, hands on her hips, face red and sweaty.

"Great effort," he said. "Really tough."

"Thanks," she said again, her eyes shut from the effort. "Needed that one. Jog with me. Okay?"

Since the separation, Ron's mother is a little more mindful of her two kids. "I spoke to Devin today," she says as Ron comes in from track practice. "He may be home next weekend."

"Cool."

She's taped some of the kids' old school photos to the refrigerator, Devin in first grade, with a buzz cut and smiling so wide that his eyes are shut; Ron in kindergarten, skinny, wearing a striped tie and a tough-guy smirk.

Most vestiges of their father are out of sight. The TV remote is in its own little metal box instead of on the coffee table. The comforter on the bed is now light blue with flowers, not the dark, solid one they'd had forever. Little touches of feminine energy have emerged—candles burning, sassy country-music women in the CD player. She's even started baking, with mixed results. Yesterday she tried a batch of muffins but something went wrong and they turned out all branny and gooey. She's happy but jittery. Her "Don't stay out too late" is less out of concern that Ron will get in trouble than a general unease at being alone at night.

"Look," she says, pointing to a framed color photo that shows him leading the state cross-country meet, about to be passed. "Isn't that great?" she says. "I finally found a frame for it downtown."

"Terrific," he says flatly.

"I'm really proud of you."

"I know," he says. Give it a few more weeks. Then there'll be a picture worth keeping.

There are rugged paths through the woods that lie between the high school track and the elementary school, where Ron can do hilly 3,000-meter circuits over dirt and grass and not have to think about dodging traffic or developing shinsplints from running on pavement. He loves to blast up those twisty, rocky inclines beneath the newly leafed maples of springtime, feeling the strain in every muscle, the forced pumping of the arms, the rising of his abdominals, the tightening in the back of his calves as bits of gravel and dirt slide backward, the shortening of his inhalations, and the gritting of his teeth. Pushing through all of that, reaching deep and finding enough to make those last few uphill strides toward a breakthrough. Then down the other side of the slope, toward the edge of the woods, breathing more deeply, opening his stride and stretching out his fingers and loping onto the grass of the soccer field and feeling his shoulders relax. Running alone. Running long and hard and loving it. Beginning another circuit. Wanting more of that pain.

Friday after practice he goes straight to his grandmother's apartment for dinner with her and his dad.

These were farm people, but they live with few hints of the past. No BLESS THIS HOUSE samplers or prints of old barns on the walls. Ron's grandmother has lived in this apartment for twenty years amid the Kmart decor and wooden furniture from Sullivan's on Church Street.

When they sold the farm there was almost no profit at all because of the back taxes, and they rented a small house near the hospital while Ron's grandfather held a job at Sturbridge Building Products and drank himself to death. That was way back, even before Devin was born. She moved here. Waited tables for a time at the diner but hated serving other people. Now she haunts the dollar store and Rite Aid. Watches soap operas. She treats Ron well—roasting chicken and making cookies and handing him a couple of dollars "just between us." She sneaks in a few sharp words about Ron's mother, assuming the breakup was his mom's fault. Not likely that she's ever discussed it with her son.

It's obvious that he sleeps on the couch out here in the living room. There's only the one bedroom, but they try to keep things tidy, at least when Ron visits.

It's a long, narrow apartment. You're in the living room when you enter from the stairs, then there's a hallway with a large bathroom on the left, then the kitchen, then the bedroom that takes up the back third of the space.

"Did you know this boy is the fastest guy around, Ma?" Ron's father is saying over dinner: pot roast with potatoes and stewed carrots.

"Not quite," Ron answers. "Not for pure speed, anyway."

"I used to be able to run like hell. Especially if the cows got loose. Remember, Ma?"

"Oh yes," she says. "Remember that time they were all out at Harry's across the way? Eating his apple trees?"

His father laughs for the first time in months. "I thought I could shoo them all back at once, but one of them was so ballsy. She was the leader. When she trotted off, the others all followed. Cows have personalities, Ron. People think they're stupid, but they're not. I could tell you the individual differences between every cow we ever had."

"He's right," Grandma says. "The young ones are like puppies, curious and getting into mischief. They'd come right up onto the porch and eat my flowers."

"They're sweet, though," Ron's father says, pushing back his glasses, which were sliding down his nose. "When I was a kid there were more cows in this county than people." He shakes his head, still wearing half a smile. "You know who's living in our house now, Ma? Two queers. I swear it. Queers with New York money. They're only here on weekends. A buddy of mine went out to fix the furnace and told me about them."

"Nothing surprises me anymore," she says. "Every time I go to the supermarket I see people I've never seen before. This town is changing right before our eyes."

They're quiet for a minute. Grandma reaches over and pats Ron's hand. "Your father is a good man, Ronald. Don't let anyone tell you otherwise."

Ron nods and digs into his plate of food. The noise level from the Main Street traffic is low, especially in the evening. You can always smell the pizza from Foley's down below, but it isn't an unpleasant or overpowering aroma.

Ron excuses himself and gets up to use the bathroom. It's kind of sad to see his dad's razor by the sink, his clothes hanging from a rack in the corner of the living room. For now he has no private space at all, but it's temporary. Most of his stuff is in storage at the Sturbridge Store-It-All out on Route 6.

There's something new on the bathroom windowsill. Ron picks it up, a little toy cow, maybe two inches tall, made of hard white rubber with large black spots painted on its flanks. The kind of toy kids played with fifty years ago.

"We playing poker tonight?" Tony asks on Monday evening. Several of them are gathered at the bench outside the Turkey Hill convenience store. "I need to win some money."

"Where's Geno?" Kevin asks. "If we're playing, it's at his house. My old man's home and he's drunk."

"He said he'd be by," Ron says. "I talked to him after practice."

It's raining very lightly, just a mist, but tonight's the first really warm night of spring and most of the guys are in T-shirts. They'll all be graduating in a month. They tend to herd up here every evening, getting Cokes and Yodels from the store but mostly sitting on the bench and watching cars go by. They share a common embarrassment, not wanting to bring these friends home and get grilled the next day at dinner about each one's families and job prospects and ambitions. They're all comfortable visiting Gene's house, though, where they can play cards in the rec room and maybe have a beer apiece and not feel like they're being watched.

Ron goes into Turkey Hill for a bottle of iced tea. When he comes out Gene has arrived, and he's talking to Kevin. Tony is chatting with Darby and Ellie—the track girls—and Ron stops cold. He caps the bottle and walks over. Darby is looking his way, hands in the front pouch of a blue Sturbridge Track sweatshirt.

"Hey, Speedy," she says, meeting him halfway.

"Hi. What are you guys up to?"

"Ellie and I decided to get some ice cream. We ran into Gene on the way over."

"We were thinking of heading to his house," Ron says. "Play some cards."

"Big bucks?"

"Little bucks. Dimes and quarters."

"Just for fun?"

"It adds up."

She's in jeans and old running shoes, and now she's standing with her hands in her back pockets, kind of leaning backward. "How was your workout today?" she asks.

"Excellent. Coach worked my ass off. He's saying I can get under nine."

"That'd be big time." She understands. Track people think in minutes and meters.

"So, what'd you do today?" he asks.

"Six-hundreds and three-hundreds. Then like two miles easy, in the woods."

She smiles at him. He notices Ellie looking their way, leaning against the back of the bench. He waves and she comes over.

"Hi, Ron," she says, her voice sounding perky and inquisitive. Something's in the air.

"Ice cream night, huh?" he says.

"Mmm, boy," she says. "We'll work it off tomorrow."

"Gotta fuel yourself somehow."

"Yeah," Ellie says. "So you guys are gambling tonight, huh?"

"Absolutely. You up for it?"

Ellie giggles. "Nah. Maybe sometime."

"Definitely," Darby says. "We've got piggy banks."

Ellie giggles again. "You dork." She gives Darby a playful shove on the shoulder. "My bank is a plastic dinosaur."

Darby shoves back. "Well," she says to Ron, "we won't hold up your game. Guess I'll see you tomorrow."

"Right. Get two scoops."

"See ya. . . . Bye, Gene," she calls. "Bye, guys."

Gene goes back in the store and comes out with a giant bag of potato chips. He and Ron fall behind Tony and Kevin as they walk up Main Street toward Gene's house.

"She's hot, man," Gene says.

"Yeah?" Ron says. It isn't really a question; he knows Darby's cute. The intonation came from wondering why Gene had pointed it out.

"Yeah," Gene says flatly. He turns his head toward Ron and squints. "You hadn't noticed?"

"Yeah, I noticed."

"You better notice, man. You better." They walk another block past the darkened stores, then Gene says, "Play your cards right, buddy. Don't overplay the hand."

On the bus ride to the league meet over in Weston, Ron rode by himself in a seat near the front and stared out the window. He was the top seed in the 1,600 and 3,200 and no one in the league had touched him all spring. Still, he had nerves; he always had nerves before a meet. So while others joked around and threw shirts at each other and Darby sat way in the back and laughed with a couple of pole-vaulters, Ron chewed on his lip and checked his gym bag twice to make sure he hadn't forgotten his racing shoes.

He could pick out her voice from time to time; she had a sweet laugh and tended to get lots of attention. So he sat there with a dual focus, or one focus and one distraction: a championship track meet and her.

He warmed up easy. His coach told him not to overextend himself in the 1,600 if he didn't have to. The battle for the team title would be close with Laurelton, and they were counting on two wins from Ron. So he jogged a couple of miles and ran a few strides, then checked in for his race and leaned against the fence to watch the girls' 400 meters.

Darby got out fast and led coming off the final turn, compact and efficient and determined, braid flying, but a tall girl from East

Pocono came on strong at the end and nipped her at the wire as Darby stumbled and fell to her knees.

The boys' 1,600 was next. Ron took a deep breath and shut his eyes and stepped onto the track. He looked around. No one in this race was at his level, but you never knew. He shot into the lead immediately and pushed through the first turn, feeling the energy of the runners in his wake, their hurried breaths and the clicking of their spikes on the track.

A guy from Laurelton stuck to his shoulder for half the race but didn't have the stamina to push it on that decisive third lap. Ron won going away.

He had a couple of hours to kill between races. He put on his sweats and drank some Gatorade and watched the hurdles final. Then he went for a walk to stay loose and look for her.

She was sitting over by the back entrance to the school, leaning against the brick wall and staring at the ground between her legs.

"Hey," she said quietly as he approached.

"Hey."

"Nice race."

"You, too."

She rolled her eyes and mouthed an obscenity. "I had her whipped," she said.

"She had a hell of a finish."

"Well, she's going to get her ass kicked in the 800," Darby said. "No way she gets me again, bro. No frickin' way."

"You'll get her," he said, but he was already backing away. "I'm gonna jog." She didn't jump up to join him. "I'll see you later," he said.

Darby just nodded, staring into space, her eyes narrowed and her mouth a tight line. Ron jogged off toward the track.

He won again easily; she didn't. She opened up a lead on the first lap and held it to the final straightaway. The East Pocono girl came firing past again and won it by a yard.

Darby didn't say a word the rest of the day. To him or to anybody. Ron might have sat next to her, taken the opportunity to show some compassion and offer some "Suck it up and work your butt off every day until there's no way that girl can beat you again" advice. Make some headway. But he didn't. The bus ride home was her turn to sit alone and glare out the window.

"Jacks over threes," Ron said, laying down his hand and sweeping the coins toward his pile. "I would say I'm on a roll, my friends."

"You suck," said Tony, who'd stayed in after getting outbluffed by a pair of tens the hand before. He set down his cards. "Three bitches."

"Hey, shut up," said Gene. "My mom's upstairs."

"I'll buy the next round," Ron said, pushing back his chair and getting up to grab some Rolling Rocks from the refrigerator. He stumbled a little. He'd had three beers already. "Okay, Geno?"

"Yeah, go ahead. Thought you had a limit during the season."

"State meet's two weeks away and I haven't had a beer since February," he said. "This is my last buzz until summer."

He opened the refrigerator and took out four more bottles. "Think your father will notice?"

"He's cool as long as we don't clean him out," Gene said. "The way you're going we might."

Ron set the bottles on the table. "Hey," he said, pointing his thumbs at his chest. "Who won two titles today? Huh?" He rolled his shoulders and gave a little dance. "Mr. Excitement, that's who."

"You're wasted, man."

"Not yet. I'm getting there."

Kevin shook his head and smirked. "Mr. Excitement?"

"Mr. Ex-*cite*-ment," Ron said, rolling his fists around in the air. "Man, I've been wound so tight all spring. I deserve this." He picked up one of the bottles and held it aloft at arm's length. "I'd just like to say what an honor it is to win this award—the Darby Rolling Rock Memorial Award for great running and dedication, and especially, especially I am proud that all my friends could be here tonight to share this great honor with me."

The boys sat back and laughed. Kevin shuffled the cards.

"I'm just sorry my father couldn't be here to see me get this prestigious reward, but he unfortunately is unavailable. So"—he stopped and took a long swig from the bottle, then wiped his mouth with his sleeve—"so, I'd like to thank the Academy and the Grammys—both of my grammys; my grampas are dead—and all you guys who unstintingly hang out on Main Street every night; you are truly an inspiration to us all. God bless us every one."

Oh my God, the room was spinning and Ron lay flat on his back, his arms outstretched and clutching the edges of the bed, and his mouth was dry as cotton. There was tension in the center of his forehead; a headache beginning to form. Oh shit, was all he could think. Oh shit.

He got up. Tiptoed to the kitchen and downed a big glass of orange juice. Brushed his teeth again. Took a leak and crawled beneath the covers. The room continued to spin until he faded into sleep.

"Ron," came his mother's voice. He opened his eyes. The room was bright with sunshine. It had stopped spinning.

"Huh?"

"You have a phone call, honey."

"Okay. Thanks."

He opened his mouth wide; the corners of his lips were sticky. His mouth tasted like a sewer. He sat on the edge of the bed for a few seconds, shaking his head. Then he went downstairs to take the phone call.

"You read the paper yet?" It was Gene.

"No, man. I'm just getting up."

"You guys get the Philly paper?"

"No. Scranton."

"The *Inquirer*'s got results from some meets down that way. That kid Daniels from Council Rock ran 9:02 yesterday."

"Geez."

"That's fast, buddy."

"No kidding."

"You got some work to do."

Ron let out his breath. "Guess I do."

"Think he drank six Rolling Rocks last night?"

"Not likely, huh?"

Ron feels like shit and knows he deserves to. But he drives to the track and stretches lightly, then sets off into the woods, fast, not bothering with a warm-up jog. He pushes up the hill and tastes bile in his throat, but he keeps going hard.

You set yourself back last night, he thinks. Daniels is running a national-class time and you're puking potato chips over Gene's back fence. You're gonna win the states? In your mind, pal, in your mind.

He's reached a flat stretch of the path now, about two hundred yards of straight firm ground. He sprints down the center of the path, the sun warm on his legs, a gentle breeze at his shoulders. He reaches a curve and slows down and circles back to his starting line.

And he hammers down the stretch again, this time in the lead, Daniels and the others on his heels. Steady and fast, holding off his rivals and easing into a decisive, killing sprint.

Again. The bell sounds for the final lap. He digs down, in control, ready to fight off any attack.

There's a puddle that covers half the path at the turn, and he pushes through, beyond it, before slowing to a jog and turning back. His vision is blurry but everything is coming around. He takes a deep breath, extending his arms at his sides and lightly shaking his wrists. He's sweating good now; he's ready to work. He wipes his hair away from his eyes and yanks his shirt out of his shorts.

He envisions Daniels moving past him, so he tucks in behind, following the steady, even gait as they accelerate toward the finish. Ron pulls even with fifty yards to go, then shifts to another gear and sprints through the tape.

Twenty-four times he runs that straightaway, cursing himself as he works to complete exhaustion. No kidding around anymore, he thinks. He drops to the dirt and does sixty push-ups.

He goes to bed at seven that evening and sleeps for twelve straight hours. He can feel himself growing inside.

Monday he's stretching by the bleachers before practice and Darby comes walking up, looking a little shy. "Hey," she says.

"Hey."

"What are you doing today?"

"Some distance," he says. "Eight or ten miles in the woods. I did a killer workout yesterday."

"Me, too."

"Yeah?"

"I came here," she says. "Did fifteen quarters. I was so pissed about Saturday. I didn't sleep at all that night."

"Tell me about it."

She laughs gently, shakes her head. She's wearing a light blue T-shirt with the sleeves ripped off. Good definition in her upper arms. "I sprinted my ass off on every one. I could just feel her coming up on me, you know?"

He nods. "No kidding. I did the same thing."

She looks surprised. "Nobody even pushed you Saturday."

"No, not directly. But there are fast people out there, Darby. Those guys who beat me in the states last fall; some kid out by Pittsburgh who's been running low nines."

"Guess we're in the same boat," she says. "I've gotta beat her at the districts or it'll haunt me all year."

"I know the feeling, believe me. Every run I take I see those two guys going past me in that cross-country race." He stares into the distance, out over the track, where people are jogging and stretching and setting up hurdles on the straight-away.

"Think we'll get 'em?" she asks.

"Yeah," he says. "I do."

"That'll be something to celebrate." She smiles, looks at him sort of hopefully. He doesn't take the hint. He swallows hard.

"I better get started," he says. "Have a good one."

Five circuits through the woods: an easy one, a hard one, a moderate one, and two kick-ass, balls-out, suck-it-up maniacal ones. Guts. Have guts. When it hurts, push through it. When you need to rest, run harder. Know that when you come off that final turn, at least two other runners will be in position to blast by you. Don't let it happen. Work so hard that no one can beat you. Lift your knees. Pump your arms. Raise that pain threshold so you can handle anything.

And then, when you're done for the day, when you're spent and you're thirsty and aching, think a little harder about this: Find some way to stop your voice from catching in your throat. A little more faith. A little less memory of earlier failures. She's waiting for you to ask her. It's no harder than sprinting through the forest.

Sports had always been the strongest connection that Ron and his brother had with their father. From first grade on they'd been encouraged, some would say pushed, to get out there and play YMCA soccer and T-ball, then progress to Biddy Basketball and junior football and Little League. Their dad coached the sports he considered tough enough to mold his little men, keeping the whistle close to his mouth during basketball practice, shouting, "Gotta box out" and "Fight through those screens" to third-grade Ron and his teammates. "Losing is not an option."

Two years of football were enough for Ron, and he turned to cross-country in middle school. By then Devin had been through the circuit—four years of junior football, a terrific year as the quarterback of the freshman team, a season on varsity special teams as a sophomore, and a growing distaste for the whole thing that made him walk away after three days of practice as a junior. It took a long time for his father to forgive that, and the resentment lingered. Devin stayed with track—sprints and jumps—but did a lot of smoking and drinking and only trained when he had to. His father couldn't comprehend that. "You've got talent," he said a thousand times. "You're wasting it."

"I don't care," Devin said a thousand times in return. "It's my life, Dad, not yours."

That was four years ago. They'd slowly noticed the change in their dad's behavior, the growing frustration. Not about Devin, that was just an excuse. Work at the factory was not very meaningful, supervising a handful of guys, dealing with petty hierarchies and paperwork and edicts from above. Getting paunchy and losing hair and working too late and needing to reshingle the house. The garage was a mess, stacks of boxes and tools and a busted lawn mower and an old sofa he needed to get rid of; no room for one vehicle, let alone two. Little Ron running *cross-country*; why not soccer, at least, if he didn't have the balls to play football?

And his wife. Out in the evenings, taking aerobics at the Y and doing volunteer work for the library. Staying up to watch the news when all he wanted to do was get to bed. That was what his life was about? He and Devin had the all-time fight and Devin left home for two years; didn't finish high school. Dad got real quiet. Finally he moved out, too.

Devin came back a year ago; got his equivalency diploma. Now he's a freshman down at Kutztown and Ron crashes there now and then on the weekends. Devin and his dad spent a couple of days in Philadelphia back in March and took in the regionals of the NCAA basketball tournament. Some of the family fractures are healing.

The Jordan Relays, in Scranton, are an enjoyable late-season meet. The dual-meet schedule is behind the athletes, and the relays are a low-pressure, Thursday-night meet the week before the districts. It's a chance to maybe try a different event, get in a tune-up race, blow off some steam and experiment.

Ron anchors the sprint medley, getting a chance to team up with Gene for the first time in a relay. The first two runners run 200 meters, the third runs 400, and the anchor leg covers 800.

Gene is fourth as he comes racing down the straightaway on the 400 leg. Scranton Prep has a slight lead over Hazleton and Meyers, and Ron is bouncing lightly at the finish, aware that he has work to do to win this thing. He'll have ten meters to make up. He'll need to get out fast.

Here comes Gene, face in a grimace, extending the baton and forcing out the word "Go." Ron reaches back, grabs the stick, and moves.

Two guys on his back. Get away from them quick. Run down those two ahead of you on the backstretch and ride in their wake for a while. The pace is very fast, way faster than in his usual races. The 800 is like an extended sprint; you never let up. The trick is to stretch out what you have, ration it over the full two laps till there's nothing left in the tank.

Around the second turn now, onto the straightaway. Gene and the others shouting, "Come on buddy, get by these guys!"

Moving out to the second lane, charging into second place, the guy from Prep a couple of strides ahead, looking fast and efficient and experienced. Taller than Ron, broader shoulders. He's run 1:55 already this season.

The bell for the final lap. This guy placed in the state meet last spring; he's tough as hell. Ron moves up on him, right off his shoulder as they barrel down the backstretch, bumping elbows as they move into the turn, both guys breathing hard, shoulders starting to tighten. Off the turn now, a hundred-meter sprint to the finish. The Prep guy veers away from the rail, forcing Ron out to the second lane.

"Lift, Ron! Lift!" he hears. And he feels it now, a bit more strength than he's had in the past, a little more fuel than he expected. And he's past the guy, an inch ahead maybe, both of them straining and groaning and on the edge of stumbling forward.

There! The tape across his chest. He beat the guy. He outsprinted the sprinter. Gene and Aaron grab him, fists in the air. "Way to go, buddy. Way to go!"

He turns, sees the rest of his teammates celebrating in the bleachers. Raises the baton toward the crowd. His coach points to his watch and nods approvingly. Had to be 1:55 or faster.

They make their way through the gate and up to join the team. Ron shakes his coach's hand, then his father's. "One fifty-four seven," his coach says.

"Beautiful," Ron's father is saying. "Tough as nails, kid. Tough as nails."

The coach pokes him on the shoulder. "Sweats on. Jog. Get yourself some fluid. Stretch very lightly."

"Got ya."

"Hell of a race, buddy. You're ready for anything."

Anything.

He caught up to her as they approached the team bus outside Scranton Memorial Stadium. "Hi," he said.

"Hey," she said, stretching out the word. "Great job."

"Thanks. You, too."

"That was the most fun meet of the year," she said.

"I know. Not so much pressure."

"Yeah. Next week, boy. That's the one."

"Right." It wasn't next week that concerned him; advancing past the districts would not be a problem. The one after that; the state meet. But after tonight, well, he felt great.

"Sit with me?" he said.

"Sure." She took a seat near the front of the bus and scooted over to the window. "Whew," she said. "First time I've relaxed all spring."

"Really?"

She shrugged. "Kind of." She giggled. "You know what I mean. Lately I've been so focused on running."

"We gotta blow off some steam," he said. "I'm taking tomorrow off. Blowing off school. Go hike in the woods. No stress; no hard work. Good set of intervals on Sunday afternoon, some light distance work on Monday and Tuesday . . . then the districts."

"Sounds great. My parents would shoot me if I cut school."

"I can get away with it," he said. "My grades are decent this semester."

"Mine, too. But they'd still kick my ass."

"Strict, huh?"

"Sort of. My father's a lawyer. They want me to go to Princeton."

"Princeton. They got a track team?"

She rolled her eyes and laughed. "Duh."

He felt his face start to glow a little and leaned back in the seat. She turned sideways to face him and pulled her knees up to her chest, wrapping her arms over her shins. "So . . . ," she said. "What about Saturday?"

"What about it?"

"You didn't say what you're going to run on Saturday. Coach said there's no practice."

"I know," Ron said. "He told me to run some easy circuits in the woods. Five or six miles."

"Oh. . . . I mean, I know I couldn't push you or anything, but if you're going easy . . ."

"You want to join me?"

"Yeah. Okay?"

"Sure," he said. "Definitely. Great."

"Like when?"

"How about ten? I don't want to get up too early."

"I'll be there."

He turned and looked toward the back of the bus, where a rowdy celebration was ensuing. He turned back and she was looking at him. She squinted slightly and cocked her head, a tiny smile on her lips.

"You busy tomorrow night?" he said.

She shook her head and her smile got brighter.

"Will you go out with me?" he asked.

"You got it."

Ron had written it all on an index card, everything he needed to know.

—Daniels: takes it out hard. Long, driving kick; 9:02

—Lancaster guy: likes to throw in some spurts, shake
 things up; X-C winner

—Pittsburgh guy: 9:05

—X factor: everybody else in the race has nothing to lose

—Me: Don't be a chickenshit. Have GUTS you son of
 a bitch.

Driving down here in the van yesterday, the small handful of Sturbridge qualifiers; holding hands with Darby, going over this race for the millionth time in his head, he'd written those notes, putting in ink exactly what he'd been telling himself all week. She leaned into him, just watching him write, no need to voice what he was feeling, wanting it more than anything. She nodded. He stared at the card.

Today was warm, sunny, perfect weather for racing. He was the only finalist of the Sturbridge athletes; Darby'd been fifth in her qualifying heat of the 400 meters.

Race time was approaching. His last high school race. The Pennsylvania state championships. His parents were here, having driven down in separate vehicles, and Devin. A carload of his teammates had driven down as well, Gene and others. They were all sitting high in the bleachers.

"I gotta warm up," he said, his voice just barely above a

whisper. His coach just nodded; they'd been over his strategy already. Ron dug in his gym bag, pulled out his spikes. Darby took his face in her hands, said nothing, kissed him lightly on his forehead, his nose, his lips. He stood and inhaled deeply, shut his eyes and opened them. Nodded in her direction and walked away.

Eight laps. Nine minutes. Who would he be when he reached the other side?

He'd won a lot of races. The league, the district; first team all-state in cross-country. That was a lot to be proud of, a lot to fall back on if he lost. And he knew that was bullshit; he hadn't proved a thing. This race would define him.

He sat on the pavement outside the locker room, stretching and staring at his training shoes. The laces were fraying; the uppers were dotted with mud from the trails behind his school, a sign of all the work he'd put in.

He got up to jog, one shoe in each hand, and saw himself fading, dropping off the fast early pace and shrinking away from the challenge. The leaders were pulling away and Ron didn't have the tenacity to stay in the hunt, didn't have enough to climb back into contention.

"Bullshit," he said aloud, quickening the pace of his warm-up. "This one is mine. I am ready right now."

He slowed to a walk, looking at the sky, letting out his breath in a huff. The kid from Council Rock was jogging nearby in a Penn Relays T-shirt, looking angry and focused.

"I'm scum if I can't handle this," Ron muttered. "I suck." He dropped his shoes, punched at the air a couple of times. "Shit," he said. "Piss. I am ready right now."

He knelt in the grass then, hands over his eyes. "Calm

down, man. Save your energy. You need every bit of strength you've got in you." He opened his eyes and took another deep breath, then slowly straightened up and extended his arms above his head. He exhaled fully and slowly. It felt good to stretch his arms and shoulders; there was new muscle there. He was strong. The sun was getting warmer. It made him looser.

"Shit," he repeated softly, picking up his shoes. He began to run slowly, his skin shining with sweat. No way to rationalize a loss in this one. It was all up to him, and nothing had ever been so clear. This was no make-believe race in the woods behind the school. This was everything he'd worked for. Everything he needed was right there inside him.

And then he saw it again. The Lancaster kid slightly ahead as they came off the final turn; Daniels coming hard on the outside. Ron, in second, digging even harder, drawing on the reserves that he hadn't quite depleted.

He turned and walked toward the track to check in for the race. He'd never felt better about anything. He loved to run in the heat.

"Report to the start."

Ron checked his spikes, the laces double-knotted and tucked in. Sixteen runners funneling toward the starting line, stripping off T-shirts, spitting toward the infield. He'd drawn lane three; he'd have to get out fast or be trampled.

As they broke from the start Ron twisted slightly to avoid the inevitable bumping. He quickly moved to the front of the pack as they came off the opening turn and into the backstretch. He knew this pace was too fast to sustain, but he wanted to stay clear of the jostling. And he wanted to set the pace, he wanted to control this one from the beginning. He felt light and strong as he led the pack.

The air was warm, each step felt good. Still a little fast, but he was finding his rhythm. His arms swung easily; each step brought him closer. Who's with me? he wondered, hearing the *gnash-gnash-gnash* of fifteen pairs of spikes behind him, feeling the steady breathing of the runners just off his shoulders.

"Sixty-three," yelled the timer as Ron finished lap one. Fast, but not too fast. Enough to string out the field, not enough to break anyone.

Daniels came up beside him late in the second lap and moved into the lead. Fine. Second place was far less frantic. Daniels's ponytail swished side to side across his shoulders; Ron could have grabbed it, they were that close.

Seven runners stayed tight through the midway point, passing in 4:26. Ron was still second. Daniels was forcing the pace, spurting now and then to thin out the pack, daring anyone to challenge him. He was nearly sprinting now, moving smoothly down the backstretch and opening a three-yard lead.

Ron opened his stride to match Daniels's speed. He felt calm and steady but was pushing near his limit. The kid in front of him looked strong as hell. Three and a half laps to go.

Daniels was five meters up at the end of the lap, and the chasing pack had dwindled to four. Ron held on to second, hurting himself with a spurt of his own but hoping to hurt the others even more. The move strung out the pack; only the black kid from Pittsburgh and a guy Ron didn't know stayed in contact. It hurt; he wanted it to. Ninety-nine percent wasn't good enough.

His fists were clenched; they shouldn't be. He shook out his hands, trying to relax his shoulders. Crunch time was approaching. Daniels held his lead, he increased it. Two laps to go. The Pittsburgh kid moved into second. Ron could hear his coach's voice, and Darby's; he could hear a thousand screaming voices. Suck it up, you son of a bitch, said the voice in his head. Suck it up *now*.

Into the homestretch, five hundred meters to go. Three of them giving chase. As a unit they seemed to be gaining on Daniels, cutting the lead back to five yards, to four.

One lap now, the state title was in reach. The brick-red rubber track, the stands a blur of color. Kick now, he told himself. Kick.

He swung wide on the turn, but his opponent wouldn't yield. Ron tucked in tighter, then moved again at the start of the backstretch. He was in second. Daniels was two yards ahead and sprinting.

Go after him, he hollered inside. Go after him. Ron dug deeper. Nothing to lose. Three of them left, nearly dead even. Sprint, you bastard. Drive. You can do this. You can win.

Half a lap to go. No air in his lungs. Find something. All those scrambles up the hills behind the track; all those intervals in the dark.

Through the turn now, into the lead. He could feel them breaking behind him, feel himself pulling away. He hugged the inside rail; they'd have to go wide to get past him. Every step was burning his lungs but every step was getting him closer. All he could see was daylight.

Into the straightaway, a hundred yards to go. He was clear of them now, a full yard in front and feeling it. No collapse at all this time, nothing but full, all-out speed.

Nothing could stop him. No one would catch him.

Every step he'd taken had been worth it.

RICH WALLACE is the acclaimed author of three novels for young adults: *Wrestling Sturbridge*, an ALA Top Ten Best Book for Young Adults, and *Shots on Goal* and *Playing Without the Ball*, both *Booklist* Top 10 Youth Sports Books. He lives in Pennsylvania with his wife and two sons.